THE HAUN[...]

BOOK TWO OF THE HAUNTING TRILOGY
BY BLAKE EDWARD ANDREW

This novel is dedicated to all the strong, fearless women throughout my life. Your inspiration continues to show the world the fierce power of femininity. The high male body count you are about to read is my return gift to you.

Oh, and always follow your dreams…

I must thank the "Mod Squad" moderators who helped me this last year while I sold book one The Haunting of Chateau de Mornay on several live social media platforms. Their volunteer help was an unexpected surprise. Without them, I would not be nearly as far in my author journey. They provided moral and technical support when the going got really tough.

Moderators
Sherry Norris, Caprice Hollis, Aliyah Berumen, Madeleine Leippi, Shawna Brown Bowers, Marjorie Brancaccio, Brittany Broom

Acknowledgments

Thank you to everyone on this list who helped finance book two with preorders, or who helped support me by subscribing to my social media accounts, or who listened to me blab about my book for an hour straight.

Abigayle Stone, Aleen Jacobson, Ali Thomson, Aliyah Berumen, Allison Vega, Amber Kennedy, Ami Jackson, Amy Russeau, Amy Wimberly, Angela Audley, Angela Koch, Angela Noble, Anna Gonzalez, Anna Stone, April Smith, Ashley Mccarty, Ben Coleman, Bill Wheeler, Bobbi Wilson, Bobbie King, Brandi Hood, Brandi Jo Marsh, Briana Bulger, Brianna Warren, Britney Parker, Britney Scott, Brittany Sink, Brittney Michael, Caelyn Resser, Caitlin Mulcahey, Casey Lynell Ward, Chelsea Henshaw, Chris Gonzalez, Christina Mccrea, Christina Rojas, Christina Sullivan, Christine Radif, Chyna Bingman, Cindy Griffin, Cindy Mischk, Clyde L Andrew, Cori Miller, Crystal Dutchess, Crystal Fillion, Cylee Welch, David Manchester, David Shurtz, Dawn Bani Domi, Deborah Ardila, Debra Newsome, Diane Woodyshek, Donna Henderson, Dorothy Barr, Dylan Conklin, Elida Sperling, Emily Wendel, Emmalee Brooks, Emylee Gussler, Erica Hilliker, Erin Doucet, Fawn Gibbs, Gaylene Salazar, Geni Bell, Geri Banuelos, Glenda Verheul, Greg Barreras, Greg Tanner, Hayley Melvin, Heather King, Heather Mylek, Holly Woodall, Honey Dy, Irma Lindauer, Isla Andrew, James Lingerfelt, Jamie Dibeler, Jennifer Tackett, Jasmine Plaunt, Jeff Edwards, Jessica Steinke, John Price, Jonathan Fryman, Joy Dye, Julie Marsh, Karen Lenhart, Katherine Bogal, Katie Hunsaker, Kayla Cline, Kayla O'Brien, Kevin Kuenkler, Kim Austin, Kim Sanchez, Kimberly Davis, Kimberly Thompson, Kristy Mullins, Krystal Steele, Larisa Devine, Leslie Twitchell, Lisa Callahan, Liz Simmons, Luna, Lynn, Madeleine Leippi, Margaret Mack, Margaret Ritter, Mark Jones, Maria Jaramillo, Mary R Hornbrook, Matthew Pennick, Mayra Lomba, Max Andrew, Melinda Phillips, Melissa Chamberlain, Melissa Feldmeyer, Michael Bjork, Michael Herbst, Michele McCammon, Misty Stockfleth, Nancy Baruth, Nicole Kelley, Nicole Perozich, Patricia Dufour, Patty Padakis, Peyton Kansley, Rachel Caschette, Rhonda Ernst, Richard McGinley, Rita Aranda, Robert Frevola, Roberta Perez, Robin Teel, Ronny Davis, Rosana Marini, Ross Nienhuis, Sara Savering, Shawna Bowers, Sherry Norris, Stacey Hite, Stefanie Hyett, Stephani Graves, Suzanne Vortman, Sydney Mabe, Tami Woodham, Tammy Putnam, Tammy Ramey, Tammy Vartanian, Tara Grantland, Tara Tinney, Taylor Smith, Tiffany Lara, Timothy Asplund, Tish Carstensen, Tori Schwartz, Tracy Nelson, Trina Reese, Valerie Ashworth, Victor Perry, Victoria H Palmer, Will Pierce, Yolanda Rangel

Cover art by George Sellas georgesellasillustrations@gmail.com

Illustrations by Eva Mout https://www.ursusart.studio/

Editing by Stephen Black

First published by Amazon KDP 2025

Copyright © 2025 by Blake Edward Andrew. All rights reserved. Printed in the United States of America. No part of this book may be reprinted in any manner without the written consent of the author.

Preface

The Haunting of Chateau de Mornay took off in a way that I did not see coming. I was a novice independently published author who hoped to sell maybe 100 copies. After one year I had sold over 6,000. I want to thank everyone for their interest in my debut novel. It truly did change my life.

Book two: The Haunting of Anna Stone continues Anna's story and was actually about 25 years in the making. When I decided to expand book one into a trilogy, I really wanted to explore the world of witchcraft. It so happened that I had begun a story about an evil witch back in college, about the year 1999. The story was around 100 pages because I never finished it.

Until now.

Sometimes you have to become the dark in order to defeat the dark. But that does not mean you cannot return to the light.

PART ONE

Chapter One

Is madness indeed a human trait, or is it simply a receptacle for evil?

-Excerpt from Dr. Richard Howard's notes

Eliza has black eyes, like staring into the darkest cave you could fathom or a black hole, light unable to escape because of the most powerful vacuum imaginable—a vacuum for souls. I felt a chill as I walked into that cave. Just by looking into her eyes, I felt as though a hand had grabbed my neck and pulled me in. I've never experienced anything like it before or since.

There is something else in that cave, something unholy. It was our first meeting. I was freezing. The room was so cold. It was July. It was at least eighty degrees outside that day. There was no air conditioner. It was her.

I'm a man of science! I can't believe I'm writing these things about her.

She had control over the room we were in. She had power over other things, too—so many things. I can't explain it. Every room that she was in fluctuated in temperature based on her mood. Just her mood! She still does it. It happens without thought to her – naturally. It is unnatural to us. She is unnatural.

That is why I can't study her anymore. She has worn me so thin. I've worked with so many killers, rapists, child molesters, and mass murderers...but she is different. She's in a whole other classification. It's a classification I don't believe we've discovered yet.

She frightens me more every day. I can't stay objective, and I feel that I'm failing as a clinical psychiatrist. I don't sleep well anymore. I can't help her. Nobody can. She was born this way, and it can't be undone. She is wholly and utterly evil.

I am writing these last words in her file today before I hand her off to another, possibly more experienced doctor.

I'm so tired. Eliza has caused my sudden fatigue just now. She knows I'm writing about her. She doesn't want me to continue. I must stop now before it gets worse.

Brockton - Three girls aged between five and eight and a twelve-year-old boy were found dead on Wednesday at the residence of Eliza Covington. The causes of death have yet to be determined, but an autopsy on the bodies is scheduled for today. Miss Covington was taken into custody and is being held on a $500,000 bond. The identities of the children are being withheld until further investigation.

Zoe's coffee grew colder as she stared at the newspaper clipping and Dr. Howard's notes. The clipping was from seven years prior, and Zoe imagined the horror those children must have endured repeatedly.

She lost her thought and stared outside the window into the blowing snow. She loved Boston; but not in winter. She had plans today but decided to scrap them because of the blizzard and her heart racing from reading the notes and press clipping.

"I'm not putting on my fucking boots and arctic gear today," she said to herself.

She looked at the research paper she was assembling for her doctorate at Harvard. What a pain in the ass. Some days, she wanted to give up, but she was too far into it to quit now. She felt like an avalanche of information was on top of her. It was impossible to get out from under it and put it into a cohesive doctoral thesis.

Zoe Rogers was a leading student researcher on the effects of sleep deprivation, sleepwalking, sleep driving, sleep paralysis, and other sleep-related abnormalities at the Division of Sleep Medicine at Harvard University. While researching, she wandered upon stories of spells and enchantments as reasons for strange, seemingly sleep-related behavior. She wanted to dismiss these tales at first but then realized she had a grand slam doctoral thesis if she pursued that avenue of sleep research. She had looked through the Harvard thesis catalog to find any related theses and found nothing close. Zoe was determined to connect science with the spells.

So here she was, led to this strange, old woman named Eliza Covington, the murderer of children who had done incredibly ghastly things. The children weren't only murdered, but their bodies were mutilated, eyes removed, teeth pulled, fingers severed, and hair torn from the scalp. Some of the mutilation was post-mortem, some not.

    The authorities eventually gathered enough evidence to search Eliza's secluded cabin deep in the woods. They procured a search warrant and discovered carnage none had ever seen before in Brockton, Massachusetts. Searches of the property's grounds recovered fifteen other skeletons, ranging from children to adults. The strangest thing about the case was that some of the skeletons were over two hundred years old. The authorities weren't able to pin the old bones on Eliza because there was no way she could have killed them. The bones were never identified. Records were scarce back in the 18th century. They chalked those deaths up to something from the past and beyond the scope of the case. The townspeople decided to have a service for the old human remains found on the property.

    Zoe had almost been dropped from her program before she found Eliza. Following the tales of amateur spellcasters and local witch stories hadn't gone over well with a previous adviser. Eliza was different, however. Zoe's new adviser told her to look into it because there was a bevy of stories and newspaper clippings about Eliza and how she may have hypnotized her victims somehow.

She pushed her medium-length brown hair behind her ears as she caught a glimpse of herself in the reflection in the window into the darkness outside. Turning to see her profile, Zoe noted her weight loss. Eliza's existence was a consuming aspect of her life, and she often lost track of time in addition to feeding herself. She frequently became laser-focused on anything she found that led to new information on the enigmatic woman. It was an obsession that Zoe had never experienced. At times, she felt fate had brought her to study Eliza.

In recent weeks, the thought of the avalanche on top of her had kept her paralyzed. It wasn't writer's block; it was rather absolute directionless boredom. Feeling out of sorts, and needing more inspiration on a cold winter night in Boston, Zoe grabbed one of her interview cassette tapes and dropped it into her home stereo. She turned up the volume and lay on the floor, wrapped in her favorite fluffy robe; her brown hair splayed out like she had just fallen from the sky.

"Eliza was a knockout. The moment I saw her, I knew I wanted to be with her forever," said the strained voice of Tom Greeley, Eliza's long-time lover. He was eighty years old when Zoe had interviewed him a year ago. Tom had a strong southern drawl, and Zoe was always captivated by listening to him talk. Tom continued, "She had such a pull on me, like a magnet. I was like a moth flying into her flame on a hot, sweaty southern summer night."

"Describe to me what she looked like, the best you can remember," Zoe asked.

"Eliza was very tall and svelte…whoa, what a body! I loved her long, wild black hair. It reminded me of a tornado. Her hair always smelled so lovely, like the way I always wanted a woman to smell."

"What year was that, Mr. Greeley?"

"I met Liza; I called her Liza, in 1946 - right after the war."

Zoe's voice grew louder on the tape, "Let it be known that this recording is being made on March 5th, 2014."

There was a ruffling of papers.

"Mr. Greeley, I'm going to show you a photo of Eliza Covington three days ago at Orrville Sanitarium."

More papers were shuffled.

There was then a crisp gasp. "How can that be?" Tom said. There was a long pause as he studied the photo.

"This can't be right. She doesn't look a day older than when I last saw her."

"When was the last time you saw her, Mr. Greeley?"

"I'd say about 1963. That's when things started going downhill for us. She was changing, distant. Liza must've been about 53 that year. But that picture, it's just not right. She looks the same."

"I've had several acquaintances of Eliza tell me that she always looks the same," Zoe said on the tape.

"How can that be?" Tom asked.

"That's what I'm trying to get to the bottom of. Here's Eliza's birth certificate, which Dr. Richard Howard dug up during her treatment. This was very hard to locate. Please read the date of birth on it."

"It says September 13th, 1910, which seems right. But the picture doesn't match that. What's going on here?"

"That is the official birth certificate. Eliza was born in Swampscott, Massachusetts, in 1910," Zoe said.

"That would make her, what...103 years old today?" Tom asked.

"Correct. Eliza is 103 years old. Look hard at that photo. Does she look 103 to you?"

"Absolutely not." There was a sigh on the recorder. "I don't believe you. This picture has to be from the 1960s. This is not Liza today. No way."

"I guarantee that this is a recent photo of Eliza. Look at the coloring on the film. That's modern photo development."

"How? I still don't believe you," Tom said, flustered.

The tape suddenly stopped, and Zoe lay alone on the floor in silence, fallen from the heavens and buried underneath the avalanche.

Chapter Two

Your breath, my dear, is missing
Lush lips I fear not kissing
Eyes so true and sapphire blue
Like a doomed ship, I am listing

It was a beautiful night, and Anna Stone could still see Chateau de Mornay's inferno down in the valley as she drove her Porsche sedan up the winding mountain road. She thought about what she had done, and the gravity of it all hit her hard. She began to cry as she thought about the loss of Luc de Mornay. She had never felt love like that in her life. Not even with her husband, Brad. Anna didn't only feel the loss in her heart of an unmatched lover, but she felt the guilt of ending his existence simultaneously. The tears fell harder. She pulled the car over on the side of the road and looked down at the orange glow far in the distance. She had to wait until she could compose herself, or she'd drive the Porsche off the mountain.

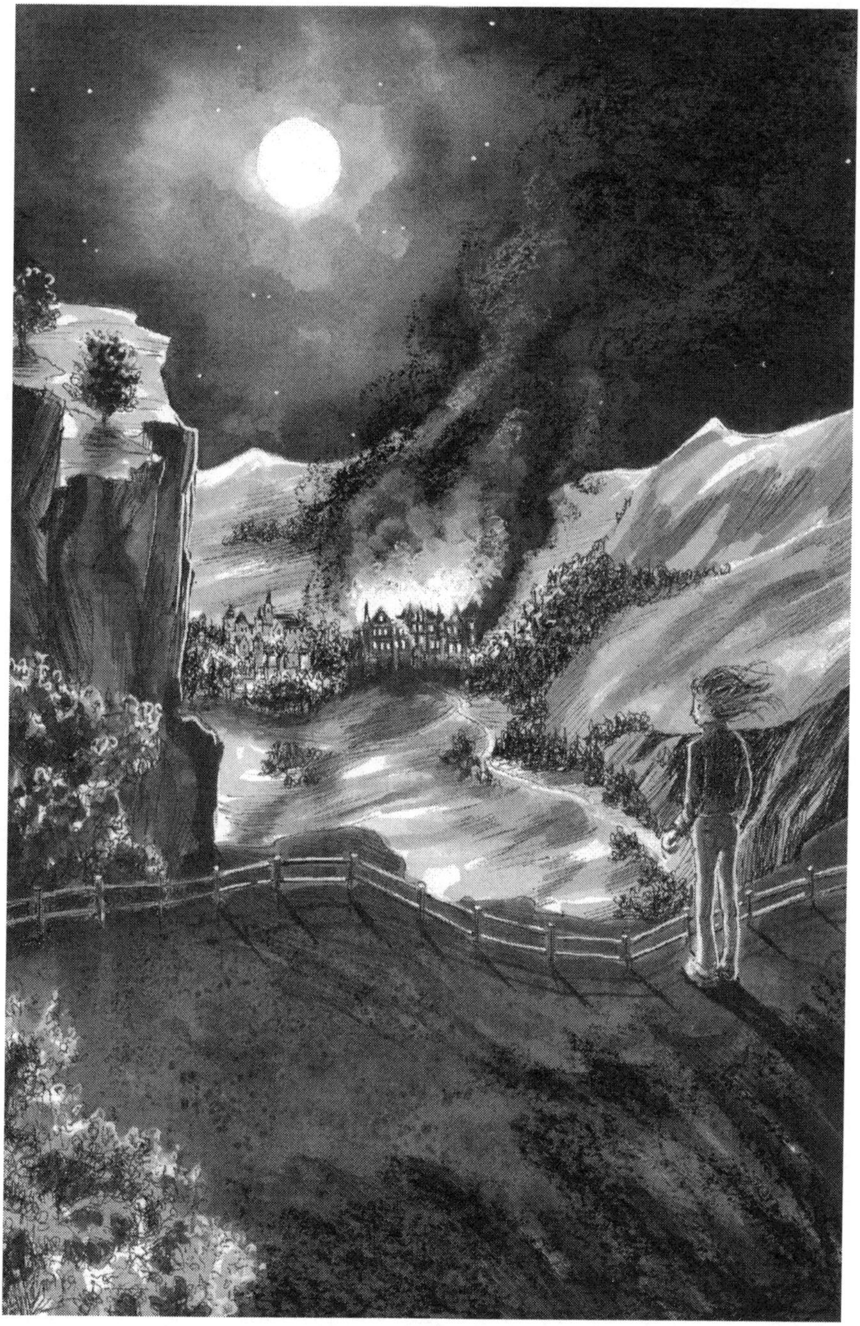

The view was astonishing. The clear night sky was full of stars while the small town of Corveau lit up like a tiny Christmas wreath hanging on a door. Anna stepped out and stood on the side of the mountain, just inside the guard rail, bundling her smoke-stained beige wool sweater closer to her body as it hung down just past her waist and covered her ever-present tight blue jeans. She watched the chateau burn as the dark smoke lifted into the night sky like a ghostly raven floating toward the moon. She wondered how similar that bloody night back in 1790 had looked with the chateau aflame and Luc's mortal body strewn in front of the building, breathing his last breaths.

What had she done? Was it the right thing? She could have left this world and remained with Luc forever, in deep love with him. The deepest love imaginable. Was that love even real? Or was it a spell put on her by Luc? It couldn't be, Anna decided, because she still felt his love within her. She felt the loss deep in her heart despite the fact that Luc de Mornay no longer existed. Or was there a chance he had survived? Maybe, she thought, but doubtful. Anna knew Luc couldn't leave the chateau. If she had learned anything from the intense experience, it was that Luc and the chateau were one. Their fates were tied together permanently. Luc and the chateau had burned together like a witch at the stake.

Witch. Anna had heard a few of Benoit's workers whisper that word as she examined their work, walking about in her nightgown. They must have seen something about her that frightened them. What about the power? The storm? She had harnessed some kind of energy to defend herself from Luc, but then also used it in attack to paralyze him and inflict a considerable amount of pain. Where did that anger come from? Where did that power come from? The moment she used it, Anna felt more potent than she ever had. It was also an overwhelming sense of joy, like her body was ecstatic to get the power out. Pure joy at the release, almost like an orgasm. And the storm that formed? That couldn't be her, could it?

She wiped the last tears away. It was time to show Etienne that she had completed her task. It was like she was Dorothy returning the witch's broom to the great Oz. She smirked at the thought as she climbed back into the Porsche.

It didn't take much longer to reach the Marchessault Castle fortress. She was already ¾ of the way up the mountain when she pulled over, and the guards at the property gate waved her in without incident. Anna again thought about the parallel to the Wizard of Oz. The guards were like that green man at the door, who let Dorothy in to see the great wizard.

As she approached the enormous door to the castle, it swung open slowly by a remote held in Etienne's hand. When she stepped in, Anna saw him waiting for her, except he didn't have a remote. Etienne motioned his hand, and the door closed behind her with a thud. She was curious about Etienne's seemingly endless powers and suddenly feared him.

"I see you brought my sword back to me," he said. The specter was dressed as an 18th century aristocrat but was much darker in countenance and overall demeanor than Luc had been. His hair was dark brown and medium length, pulled back behind his ears. His brow hid the dark hazel eyes from the living world. "And my condolences for your loss. I know he was important to you. I know the power he had over you."

"He did have power, but there was also love, and you know it," Anna said. "He's gone now, and yet I still feel intense love for him. I miss him." She wanted to withhold her true feelings from Etienne, but her heart hurt too much not to show her pain.

"I understand, and again, I'm sorry for your loss," Etienne said as he bowed before her. Anna did not expect this gesture based on her past experiences with him. He had proven himself unscrupulous in one moment but now tender in the face of loss. However, Anna knew that Etienne rejoiced inside, for the final chapter in the book of the de Mornay family was over.

"Yes, I do rejoice inside, Anna, but I'm also respectful to a degree," he said with a sly smile.

"I forgot that you're in my head all the time, just as Luc was," she replied.

"Not like Luc. One-hundred times stronger. I doubt there's any thought you could conjure while in my castle that I can't detect. It's my curse, just as Luc had his. If I could find a way to heaven, I would give anything for it," Etienne said as he made the sign of the cross on his chest.

He would give anything to go to heaven. Etienne, the monster who had murdered Luc and his family and masqueraded as a descendant of his own family to avoid detection in his ruse of dominion over the de Mornay memory.

Behind the darkness of his heavy brow, Anna saw him glance down at his sword in her hand. The sword that had killed Luc so long ago on that night of terror. The sword that Etienne had attempted to deceive her with. She held it by the dull blade instead of at the hilt, showing Etienne that she meant no harm.

"What will happen if I give this to you?" she said.

"Nothing except for my deepest gratitude for destroying Chateau de Mornay for me and ridding us of the treacherous leech that was Luc de Mornay."

A large thump in her heart as Etienne defamed her former lover. She hated Etienne for it but had to hide it from him as much as possible. Anna handed the sword to him. She wondered if it was a mistake. She might need it as a weapon against him. Then she glanced around and saw the copious amount of weapons on the walls and thought against it.

"Thank you," he said as she laid it on his open hands…the hands of a ghost like Luc, but far more powerful. Etienne examined it. "It's good to have it back." He looked at Anna and smiled wide. "Now for your reward."

"You promised my freedom," Anna said, remembering how Etienne had held her captive briefly.

"I did, and it's granted. You're released," he said with a wave of his hand, like he had let go of some silly force field around Anna.

Anna appeared bashful, "What if I told you I wanted to stay here?" Her vengeance would have no bounty if she departed.

Etienne's eyes squinted. He knew she had something on her mind. "Why would you want that?"

"I'm not staying forever, Etienne. I just need to rest and recover. I feel weak after the confrontation."

He knew she was up to something, but Etienne complied because he liked games. "Of course. You can stay as long as you'd like. You can have anything you need. My resources are boundless. Likely more than that of your actor husband."

Brad. With all the commotion, she had barely remembered him. He was likely on his way but would think that Anna perished in the fire. She had left her cell phone in the chateau. She never considered getting it or anything else vital once she started the fire. The local fire brigade and authorities would think that she had died there as well. She needed to rest and think of how to handle everything that had occurred.

"Please, come in and make yourself at home. Is there anything you need?" Etienne said as he waved for a servant to tend to Anna.

"I just need a bed. I'm exhausted."

"Of course. I'll have a room prepared immediately. I'll give you the biggest quarters in the castle. You earned it. You've made me extremely happy."

Etienne nodded at the servant, dressed like a modern butler who looked in his forties. The servant walked away to do his duty.

"Please sit with me and have a cognac while your room is prepared," Etienne said. "I know you're tired, but we have much to discuss."

He led the way to the expensive leather chairs, and Anna plopped down, completely spent. She was again puzzled about a ghost imbibing but was too tired to care. She had seen enough strange recent events for a lifetime. Cognac and specters mixed. She got it.

"Yes, I can taste the cognac, Anna," Etienne said with a smile. "I don't drink this just for appearances. Unlike Luc, I am whole and essentially human…except for this accursed immortality."

Anna sighed at his cockiness. She was already tired of his presence.

"I'm glad you decided not to follow Luc into Hell," he said, staring at Anna with his forlorn eyes. "I would have hated to see such talent go to waste."

Anna sighed. She was nearly fed up with the whole night and the misadventure she had just experienced. She wasn't sure she could take much of Etienne's shit tonight either. "What talent, Etienne?" Her eyes rolled as she said it.

24

Etienne leaned forward with youthful purpose. "I saw what you did to him. I was there, watching you, observing. I was without form, of course, because I did not want to interfere in any way."

"Would you have let me jump?" she asked, testing the specter to see if he had been present when she had made her fateful choice.

He took no time to answer. "Yes."

"That's reassuring. And here I thought you were my ally."

"Allies only because we had the same goal - his death and your freedom. My only question was, 'Which freedom would she choose?' I left the choice completely to you. And yes, I would have let you fall to your death."

"Thanks," Anna scoffed. Her blonde hair was messy and dirty from soot, ash, sweat, and tears. She knew that Etienne had the power, even as a spirit, to leave his castle in corporeal form and quickly stop her from freely falling to her death or Luc throwing her off the 5th-floor balcony of the chateau.

"Perhaps now is not the time, but we need to talk about what you did to Luc," Etienne said before sitting forward in his chair in excitement again. "You froze him and cracked his material form into pieces like a crushed porcelain vase, Anna!

It was fascinating and exhilarating to watch. I haven't had that much joy in decades!"

Anna's eyes were closed.

"Anna?" he said as he leaned toward her.

The poor, weary Anna had passed out moments after sitting down. She felt safe for the first time in seemingly days sitting across from Etienne, but her body and mind were beyond fordone.

Etienne sat back, and the leather chair squeaked. "Rest, Anna. You will need it for what is to come."

"Mon amour, I am here."

Anna found herself walking in the enormous front garden of Château de Mornay. It was the garden as it looked in the late 1700s before the revolution came. She smelled the freshly bloomed cornucopia of flowers and greenery. The air was cleaner somehow back then. Why was she here?

"Mon amour, I am over here."

She heard Luc de Mornay's voice and looked toward it. There he was, standing on a scaffold, painting. He was painting the piece that hung in the Corveau museum that she had visited. There he was! Luc was dashing and handsome with a blue coat, white skin, red hair, and those piercing, devastating bright blue eyes. Anna's heart skipped upon seeing him again. She walked toward him and realized she was wearing a dress from the 1700s. The trail of the dress dragged on the ground. It was something she would never wear. She hated dresses. Why was she here? Why now, at this moment? Was she dead and now Luc's eternal lover?

Luc paused and stared at Anna. "Mon amour, you are why poetry exists."

Anna blushed with a shy smile. "Thank you, Luc."

"Wait until you see what I'm painting, mon amour. It will take the breath from your lungs."

It was the perfect day. Anna didn't want it to go. If it were a dream, it was the most real one she'd ever had. The overwhelming visceral sensations made her feel drunk with joy. She felt deep happiness for the first time since falling for Luc. And there he was. Luc. Her lover, forever, and alive again.

Anna was content to be dead. She hoped it was death that kept her with Luc. Just as she was about to see the painting, she awoke.

She opened her eyes. Indeed, it had been a dream. The residue of joy and love with Luc lingered after awakening, just as some powerful dreams do. The dream hangover also gave her a serene feeling of peace, like she had died with Luc and it felt…right.

Anna realized she was in the most comfortable bed she'd ever been in. Black satin sheets entrapped her with luxury like a mother's warm embrace, which she had never experienced. The pillow was the softest, cool on her face and refreshing. Anna was in a king-canopy bed. She examined it with sleepy eyes and noticed dark wood posts, glossy with varnish. A thin silk sheet surrounded and hung from the posts, draping down like a bride's veil.

The room was enormous and very dark. The windows were shuttered from the outside, so she had no sense of the time of day. Intricate walls of dark wood lined the room. Large rugs covered parts of the stone castle floor as she pulled herself up for a better look. She noticed a small fire shrinking down in the fireplace. Anna's eyes caught a priceless burgundy sleeveless gown at the end of the bed, no doubt tailored to her by some type of power of Etienne. She would gladly wear such a remarkable gown.

The dream. It had been so real. Was it Luc trying to reach her from wherever he was now? He must be so alone.

But then Anna wanted to cheer herself up, believing that Luc was reunited with Louisa and their two children, Phillipe and Claudette…and their unborn child, all struck down that night by Etienne and his soldiers. Maybe it was some kind of heaven for Luc? She didn't believe in Heaven or Hell the way Etienne did. The dream was something far beyond those two worlds. The weight of her recent losses hit her again. Audrey, Brad, Luc…when would they end? When could she begin a path to happiness, and what would that look like now? How could Brad take her back, or was he even the same Brad she had fallen in love with so long ago?

However, Luc reigned supreme in her heart at that moment. Anna knew it was wrong that she had cheated on her husband with a ghost, but the love of Luc de Mornay lingered inside her heart. She desired more than anything to see him again.

But she had killed Luc. Chateau de Mornay would soon be nothing but smoldering ashes because of her. Her home was gone. Her marriage was likely over. Anna wanted to stay in bed forever.

Chapter Three

Zoe awoke to her cell phone ringing. She grabbed it and noticed the clock said 3:15 am. It was a number she had on her phone.

"This is Zoe."

"This is Dr. Howard. Can we meet somewhere?"

Zoe heard the terror in his voice. Her interactions with him had always been composed and professional, but he had rapidly changed. He was in distress.

"We can meet in the coffee shop near the sanitarium like last time," she said.

"No! That's too close," he barked back. "Can I come to your apartment?"

Usually, Zoe would think of this as a ploy to get into her pants, but she knew Dr. Howard wasn't that kind of man. "Yeah, that will be fine."

"You live pretty far from her, don't you?"

"Far from whom?"

"Her," he said, followed by a disconnecting beep.

Dr. Howard looked like a drug addict on the street, worn and strained, his eyes red and darting everywhere. "She can hear me, when I'm near her," he said while he grasped his coffee cup with two hands, as if it were the holy grail itself. Zoe couldn't blame him for needing heat in the chilly Boston weather. She had thrown on a sweatshirt (likely an old boyfriend's), a pair of sweatpants, and started a pot of coffee before Dr. Howard showed up. She heard his car screech to a stop on the street, sliding on asphalt and ice at 4 am. She unlocked the door and let him into her apartment quickly before any heat could escape.

Before they sat down, Zoe poured him a cup of fresh coffee. "Tell me what's going on," she asked.

He took a sip, sighed at the welcoming warm goodness, and said, "after meeting you at the hospital, I returned to my office." He paused and his mind went adrift, quite uncharacteristically for him. "After some time, one of my assistants rushed in quite upset. She had a small video cassette and immediately put it into the player in the corner of my office. She didn't say anything. We both watched as the screen lit up." He paused and looked into Zoe's eyes intensely. "I have the tape with me. I need to show you."

Zoe's heart instantly went into overdrive. She couldn't believe she was about to see Eliza for the first time on video or in person. It had been a long time coming.

Dr. Howard handed her the small videotape. It was a standard closed-caption format that worked with most equipment. Zoe walked over to her system, set it up, and hit play.

The video came to life. It was Eliza's padded cell. Her face was shrouded in a strange shadow cast by who knows what. There was enough light in the room to fill a basketball arena, yet her face was hidden behind her dark, greasy hair and a mysterious shadow. The walls and the floor of her cell were white. The light must have been so tortuous to the poor woman. Maybe they did that intentionally?

Eliza wore a white hospital gown as she stood in the middle of the cell. Her arms were at her sides. There was a slight audio hiss. After a few minutes of watching her standing there, motionless, Zoe grew uneasy and hit the fast-forward button. Even at high speed, Eliza didn't move an inch. Zoe watched the time stamp counter increase to ten minutes. No movement.

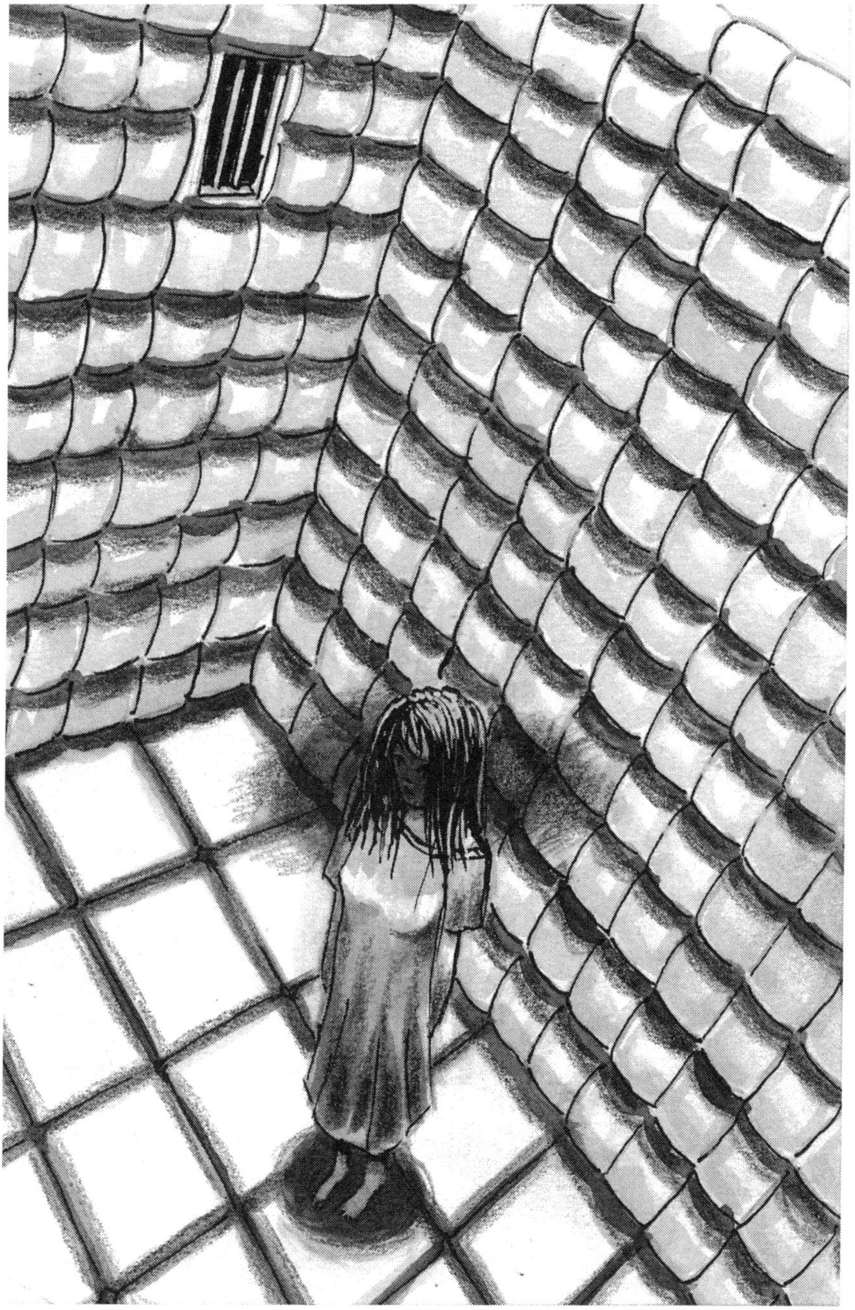

Then, a slight gesture of Eliza's hand made Zoe change it back to average speed. At first, it was minimally audible, but it grew louder. Zoe's heart raced. She couldn't believe what she heard. It was a child laughing. Eliza was still motionless with her face in a shadow. The child's laughter grew louder and then more childrens' laughing voices filled the room. The children sounded like they were playing a game and singing a song. Zoe felt a chill and looked over at Dr. Howard, whose eyes were glued to the television. He looked like he was about to cry.

"There must be something wrong with the audio," Zoe said, trying to rationalize the strange behavior.

"No," he said. "There is only one microphone in the room, next to the camera high in the corner. It's impossible to manipulate."

Zoe watched Eliza's motionless form as the children's voices haunted her with mirthful chatter. How could it be?

Suddenly, Eliza lifted her arms and began twirling as she laughed and danced with the unseen children. The scene froze Zoe's blood.

"Have you seen her do this before?" she asked.

"No."

Zoe heard the sheer terror in Dr. Howard's voice. His response was a whisper and a cry at the same time. Her gaze stayed on him for a few moments of concern before looking back at the frightening television.

Eliza continued to dance around the room to the children singing, child-like in her movements. She appeared to be dancing in a group as she carefully weaved around imaginary obstacles. Occasionally, she would motion her hand like she was patting a child's head.

"Here it comes," Dr. Howard said. "Go ahead and hold down the fast-forward button again."

Zoe did what he suggested. She watched the timestamp speed up as Eliza's dancing matched the fast speed. Then, she began slowing down. As the tape and timestamp speeded at double time, Eliza appeared to be dancing normally.
"What the hell? She must be moving so slowly to do that," Zoe said. "Why would she?"

Suddenly, Eliza did something that made Zoe step back. Her head turned slowly to the camera in the upper corner of the room. The shadow veil dropped from her face and revealed a lovely, young, smiling woman, much younger than her usual appearance of a woman in her forties…or 103. Her teeth gleamed in the bright room. She stared motionless and unblinkingly at the camera with her terrifying smile. Zoe watched as the counter flipped faster. One hour. Two hours.

Three hours. Four hours. No movement. Just her bone chilling smile staring at them.

Chapter Four

A very tired Anna sat on the leather couch across from Etienne, her legs crossed elegantly in the gown as she sat with her back straight. She was concerned about wrinkling the fine fabric, despite it likely not being real. She had slept for so long, yet was still exhausted from recent days. Etienne stared at her, his dark eyes hidden by his heavy brow. She still caught herself in disbelief that she had been conversing with ghosts that acted perfectly like real humans—not just talking but also touching and making love.

The silence became awkward. Anna didn't know whether to speak first or allow Etienne to. Etienne sat rigidly in his chair, the light of the fire dancing in his eyes.

"I trust that the gown fits?" he asked, his eyes wandering over her body.

"Yes. It is perfect. Thank you," Anna replied.

"While you're in my castle, your beauty demands a more elegant look," he said. "We can't have you wearing a dirty sweater and denim. If you'd like, I can have your hair done."

Anna scoffed at him. "No thank you. Were you going to conjure a hairdresser too?"

"You are in a house of God, and I am his hand. Everything I do is divine. I expect you to appear as an angel," Etienne said.

"A house of God? Etienne, you're a killer," Anna said with a tinge of accusation.

"Anna, do you not perceive the grandeur of creation?" he said. "The very essence of the world speaks of a divine hand, an omnipotent God who weaves our fates with purpose. There is a design inherent in the chaos that surrounds us. Even my own actions, as small as styling your hair with a snap of my finger, is God's will."

Anna leaned forward, a shadow of doubt etched upon her brow and her strength returning. "Design? Or mere illusion? If God governs the Earth, His ways are mysterious, leaving us to navigate a labyrinth of suffering and despair. Look around you! The smoldering chateau outside reflects the turmoil within our souls, and yet you insist on attributing it to a higher power?"

Etienne's voice rose, an emotional plea. "But the chateau itself is part of the divine tapestry! Each storm, each act of nature, is imbued with significance. It is through hardship that we grow, that we come to know His will. To deny this is to embrace a void, an abyss devoid of meaning."

Anna shook her head, her dirty, sooty blonde hair cascading over her shoulders, just the way she wanted it. "The void is precisely what I acknowledge. The world is a place of chaos, where events transpire without reason. I cannot surrender my intellect to blind faith. The notion of a benevolent deity feels like a cruel deception, a comfort for the weak."

Etienne's eyes narrowed, his expression a mix of disappointment and concern. "You reject the very notion of hope, Anna. Without it, what remains? We are but fleeting shadows, lost in a vast expanse. To believe in God is to embrace the possibility of redemption, to find solace in the storms that besiege us. Redemption is my only hope when I am no more."

Anna's voice softened, revealing the vulnerability beneath her bravado. "And yet, the same storms they view as trials can also be seen as capricious, indifferent forces that mock our struggles. If God exists, then He allows the innocent to suffer, just as Luc's children did! Where is the grace in that?"

Etienne leaned closer, his sincerity palpable. "It is not grace that we seek in suffering but understanding. Perhaps the suffering of the innocent is part of a greater lesson that we may not yet comprehend. We are mere mortals, striving to grasp the unfathomable. I followed God's hand when I killed them."

Anna's heart quickened at his words, a flicker of something deeper igniting within her. "Yet, can you not see the danger in such thinking? To excuse the horrors of the world or your actions as divine lessons is to risk complacency. We must confront the chaos, not hide behind the veil of faith."

Etienne's brow furrowed, the firelight illuminating his frustration. "But what, then, is your remedy? If you deny the existence of a higher power, what fills the void? Is it not despair that you court, rather than liberation?"

Anna felt the weight of his gaze, the intensity of his passion urging her to reconsider. "I seek truth, Etienne. A truth that exists without the need for divine justification. I would rather face the chaos as it is, raw and unfiltered, than construct a comforting illusion to shield me from reality."

Etienne leaned back, resignation etched across his features. "So, you choose to walk the path of isolation and Hell, rejecting the embrace of faith that has comforted humanity for centuries? Can you not find beauty in belief, even if it is not absolute?"

Anna pondered his words, the energy crackling between them like a storm. "There is beauty in connection, but it must stem from honesty. I refuse to anchor my life to a belief that may crumble under scrutiny. We are creatures of the earth, bound by our experiences, not celestial dictates."

Etienne's voice softened, an almost pleading note entering. "And yet, is it impossible to find strength in our experiences and the belief that there is more? That our lives are part of a grand narrative, written by a benevolent hand?"

Anna's gaze drifted to the window, the dark clouds swirling ominously. "What if that narrative is but an illusion? What if we are the authors of our own stories, free from the constraints of a divine script? In chaos, we can find our truths, forge our destinies."

Etienne felt a surge of frustration and admiration for her fierce independence. "And yet, in your quest for autonomy, do you not risk losing the very essence of what it means to be human? We long for connection, for purpose, and perhaps it is in faith that we find our place in this chaotic world."

Anna turned to him, her eyes fierce and defiant, hopeful for an accord. "Then let us forge a new understanding that acknowledges our struggles and the beauty of our existence without the need for divine justification. Let us seek meaning in each other, in our shared—humanity." She trailed off clumsily, remembering that she was talking to a spirit who was human no more.

Etienne's voice, low and resolute, cut through the tension when he spoke. "Then let us navigate this storm together, Anna. Let us confront the chaos as allies, not adversaries. Perhaps we can discover a truth that transcends our beliefs."

Anna's heart raced at the promise in his words, the flickering firelight reflecting the uncharted territory of their connection. "I will stand beside you, Etienne, but only if we can acknowledge the lingering shadows. Let us not pretend that we have all the answers."

Suddenly, Etienne raised his hand and snapped his fingers with a wily grin. The next instant, Anna opened her eyes to pain in her wrists and her body was cold. She shivered as she awoke to realize she was in an empty, dark stone room with bars as a door. It was a cell. The sharp pain from her wrists came from them being shackled to a stone wall, the chains only two feet long, from where her limp body had hung for possibly hours. The cold bit at her body because she was completely naked.

"Etienne?" Anna said in a whisper because her energy was unexpectedly low. "Help." She looked around and only heard dripping water from centuries of moisture cascading down the cell's stone walls. The cell smelled of wet rock with minerals vital enough to overtake other scents. Her hair hung in her face, dirty and wet. She could not move it because she was too weak to shake her head like she usually would toss her hair to the side. Her blue eyes burned from tears that she was unable to wipe away.

"Don't mock me by trying to earn my favor or come to some kind of agreement on an age-old question. I'm not stupid." Etienne paused for a few moments. "I know what you are, Anna." His voice boomed throughout the cell, but she knew he was not nearby. "I've known since I met you the first time you came to my castle. I felt it. Then I saw what you did to Luc easily, which was even more proof."

Anna was so weak and tired that she didn't want to reply. Her anger toward Etienne was only a tiny, kindled flame inside her, not strong enough to curse him. She had no idea how long she'd been hanging naked by the chains, but her stomach growled, and she had to pee. She could barely keep her eyes open from the burning, salty tears. "Why, Etienne?" her weak voice squeaked.

"Why? Because I know what you're capable of. I fear it has to do with the legend we've heard about in this area since childhood. The legend existed even before my parents were children."

"What are you talking about?" Anna whispered slowly, her voice too weak. But she knew Etienne heard her and also could read her mind. She was entirely at his bidding.

Etienne began: "When I was a young boy, I heard the tale of the mountain witch for the first time. In Japan they have the yamauba, a similar tale, but in this region of France she is known as *la femme serpent*, or the serpent woman. They say she is the same Greek myth of Pythias, whose serpent Apollo slew at Delphi. Why she is here in this region of France, we do not know. But I swear to you, Anna, I saw her once in the mountains near here. By then, I was in my teenage years, and the fear I had harbored as a young boy of wandering alone in the mountains had disappeared. My parents used her as a way to make me behave. They'd say she took young children if they did not listen to their parents' commands. I was terrified of her while I was young, but that fear was gone as a young man, until the day I spotted her. I enjoyed climbing and following the wild mountain goats as they made their daily crossing of a rather steep section not far from my family castle. There was mist, as always at that height, but upon pulling myself up to a small landing to rest, I saw a figure in black perhaps fifty meters above me. It was her. I felt it. She wore a tattered black cloak, and her black hair shimmered from the moisture of the thick fog. I simultaneously saw her alabaster face; sadly strained and wrinkled, yet beautiful. It was like she had been a fair maiden once and some dark force had overtaken her heart and turned her into a monster. These thoughts came to me as I stared at her. They may have been her thoughts telling me of her sad history. I do not know." There was a pause. "However, I do know you are connected to her. I haven't felt like this since I saw her so long ago. It's hard to explain what it is. I suppose I would call it a feeling of impending doom. A constant fear that I can't shake off. You are connected to her for some reason. Your presence here in this region, even within Chateau de Mornay, is no coincidence. It is your fate, and I'm going to keep you here until I learn more about you."

"Why am I naked and starving, you goddamn asshole?" Anna spit out the words with all her quiet might.

"Because witches are the spawn of the Devil. You deserve nothing more, heretic."

She shook her head and passed out.

Chapter Five

Zoe awoke to a random car horn outside. She had been a shut-in for two days since watching the video of Eliza for the first time. She had been watching it over and over, trying to deduce even the slightest clue or catch a random detail that would have made the strangeness of Eliza's behavior more believable. Zoe felt no better. Her head swam even more with each viewing. She hadn't showered nor eaten much. Takeout had been her sustenance in the cavern she shared with Eliza.

She prepared a pot of coffee to begin feeling human again. This had been her pattern each day, to no avail. Her humanity seemed to be slipping away the further she dove into the behavior of this strange woman who never seemed to age.

Zoe made her coffee like she preferred - with cream and sugar - lots of both. She wore a robe and sat down before her laptop to read the local daily news. She scanned through the usual bland bigger news titles until one caught her eye…

RENOWNED LOCAL DOCTOR FOUND DEAD

BOSTON - *Doctor Richard Howard died from a sudden heart attack at Orrville Sanitarium yesterday. He was best known for his book "The Fire Inside".*

The article continued about his family and planned services, but Zoe couldn't breathe. "What the actual fuck?" was all she could get out as tears came to her eyes. She had JUST seen him! She broke down and cried, mostly from exhaustion, but also this latest piece of tragic news that her mind couldn't make sense of. She allowed herself to cry and wiped her tears and nose with her old robe sleeve.

Once composed, all she could think of was calling the sanitarium. She had a direct line to Dr. Howard's office. She picked up her cell and selected his office in her contacts.

"Hi, Zoe. I was going to call you today," Dr. Howard's assistant Rachel said. Zoe mainly had worked with her while trying to get to Dr. Howard early in her research.

"I knew his health wasn't good, but this?" Zoe said, still sniffing and red in the eyes.

"I can't talk about it now, Zoe." Rachel's voice grew more quiet on the other end. "I'm sure you understand why."

"Uhh…I'm not sure I do, but okay," Zoe responded.

"Dr. Roth is now seeing his patients."

"Fuck!" Zoe shouted. She had tiptoed so carefully for so long just to get into contact with Dr. Howard and now she would have to start over. She felt a ping of selfishness momentarily. A man had just died.

"Zoe, I'm so sorry."

"No. Shit, I'm sorry, Rachel. All I can think of is my research."

"I understand. Dr. Roth isn't as forthcoming with information as Richard was. You may be at a dead end, no pun intended. Jesus I can't believe I just said that."

"No, it's okay. I'm sure you're shook," Zoe said through more sniffles.

"Zoe, can I come see you when I get off work later?" Rachel asked. It wasn't unexpected. She had said she couldn't talk much while at work.

"Of course. I'll text you my address. I'll be here when you're ready."

Rachel rushed in the moment Zoe opened the door. Dr. Howard's assistant was tall with a quiet beauty hidden behind a world of endless work in an insane asylum. Her hair was pinned up and makeup that may have been there was now missing surely due to her crying. Rachel reached into her bag and pulled out a video tape.

"Ah, more of these," Zoe said as she smiled and took it.

"Then you saw the last one? Richard was here?"

"Yes, he was beyond distraught. He didn't tell you he was coming to see me?"

Rachel frowned. "No. That's highly unusual for him. But given his recent state, I'm not surprised."

Zoe walked over to the player, dropped the tape in, and took a deep breath. What odd behavior would she see now?

"I have to warn you. This is…" Rachel started saying as Zoe cut her off.

"I know. I saw the last one."

"Okay, just be ready. Let me say a few things before you hit play. I told you that Dr. Roth took over his patients. I assume you haven't met her?"

"I haven't."

"She's…different. Some say prickly, while others say bitch."

Zoe scoffed. "Okay."

"She's not gentle in any way. I'm concerned about her taking Eliza as a patient. Richard had enough sense to be careful and caring with Eliza. Roth does not. Anyway, I can't say anymore until you watch this."

Zoe hit play.

It was Eliza's cell again. She was sitting alone on her bed with her feet on the floor. Her face was once more obscured by a mysterious shadow, although there was much more light this time. Her dark, curly hair cascaded down the front of her hospital gown to her chest. Zoe knew of her resounding beauty, but the woman she saw was tired and drawn from years of being researched in an insane asylum.

After a few moments, Dr. Howard walked in. He brought in a chair, which they don't leave because they'd had trouble with Eliza and metal chairs. Dr. Howard pulled up the chair and sat about five feet from Eliza. She showed no change with his presence.

He had a clipboard and began asking her questions. Even after turning up the volume, Zoe couldn't understand what he was saying. He was waiting for responses from Eliza, but there was no indication of any. It was obvious that he was just doing his usual rounds with her. The questions were likely the same ones every day. Zoe knew that Eliza rarely responded due to heavy sedation.

Suddenly, Dr. Howard jolted up, like something had hit him. He dropped the clipboard and slumped forward.

"That's probably the heart attack," Zoe said. Rachel gave no response.

Eliza showed no change, even as Dr. Howard slipped off the chair and collapsed on the floor. They watched the time counter go by.

"You can fast-forward this part," Rachel said.

Zoe did so and the counter zipped past. Ten minutes. Twenty minutes. Oh, this again?

"How far should I go?" Zoe asked.

"Five hours," she replied.

"All that time and they didn't know he was gone?"

Rachel ignored her. "When you reach the five-hour mark, hit play again."

After thirty seconds of watching the video feed on fast forward, Zoe returned it to normal speed. Nothing had changed in the room.

"Turn up the volume here," Rachel said.

Zoe did so. They heard giggling. It kept growing more intense. It was coming from Eliza. They then saw her body quivering as the laughter got louder. Then it progressed to a deeper laugh - almost like a man's. She began whispering in a deep, throaty voice. The two women had trouble making it out, so Zoe raised the volume.

"Dark. It is coming. The Dark is coming," Eliza's guttural, horrible voice said, turning to normal volume. The shock of the sound made the women jump.

Zoe turned toward Rachel. She just shook her head. Goosebumps all around.

Then it happened. Dr. Howard started moving.

"He's still alive!" Zoe shouted as she pointed at the screen. Rachel didn't waver and Zoe knew that was not a good sign.

They watched as Dr. Howard pulled himself up from the ground. His coordination was poor - he was weakened and struggling. Zoe feared what Eliza would do to him. Her heart was racing as if she had been running the Boston marathon. Dr. Howard started crawling, pulling himself along the floor with his arms—like his legs were paralyzed. They dragged behind him like a half-crushed lizard clinging to life on a desert highway. He slowly crept up to Eliza and pulled himself up onto the bed. She opened her legs, and he slid down on his knees in front of her.

"I'm going to be sick," Zoe said.

They watched in horror as he ripped her hospital gown and pulled it down, revealing her breasts. Eliza tilted her head back as Dr. Howard began aggressively biting her neck and then slid down to her breasts. He caressed and sucked on them, and she started moaning in a low voice, even lower than before.

"Oh my God. How can he do that?" Zoe asked. She felt queasy. Rachel was transfixed on the screen, seemingly hypnotized.

Eliza's moans became louder as Dr. Howard grew more aggressive. Eliza started rubbing his back and running her hands through his hair. He then slid down further. Rachel turned away. Zoe also wanted to, but she was compelled to keep watching simultaneously.

Dr. Howard bent down and pulled up her gown. He reached his hand between her legs, and she let out a ghastly howl of monstrous ecstasy. He was rough with her, rubbing her harder and harder. He bent down further and put his face between her spread legs. She moaned so loud that the speaker distorted. Her hands grasped the bed on both sides of her and it rattled violently. Eliza had a full orgasm.

After she was done, Eliza pushed Dr. Howard's face away with such force that he flew back, knocking the chair over. He laid motionless in a heap on the floor, his face glimmering in Eliza's wetness. Zoe watched Eliza sitting there with such contempt for the insane woman. She was naked and a shambles, her hair a mess from the intensity of the sex.

Zoe was sick. She was angry at Dr. Howard as well. He's her doctor. How could he do that?

Eliza began laughing again in her childlike way. The whole scene was beyond disgusting.

"You can stop it now," Rachel said.

Zoe took one last glance at the screen - his unconscious body on the floor, hers post-sex. She shut it off.

"What was that?" Zoe asked.

Rachel gave out a huge sigh. "I'm still not sure what that was."

Zoe walked over to a cabinet and pulled out a bottle of whisky. She uncapped it, poured two full glasses, and handed one to Rachel.

"Who needs a fucking drink?" Zoe asked rhetorically.

"What I didn't tell you," Rachel said after cringing from the first sip, "was that this video is from two days ago. We only let the news out to the press yesterday about his death because we're still trying to figure out what happened. The police are involved, too."

"Shit," was all Zoe could get out as she took a big drink.

"I was able to copy the tape. This one's yours," Rachel said.

"I'm almost ashamed to keep it here."

"The other thing I didn't tell you is that they already carried out an autopsy on Richard."

"And?"

She took a big swig. "He didn't die from a heart attack. It was a sudden brain aneurysm. A big one."

"Okay," Zoe said, knowing Rachel had more to say.

"And..." Rachel trailed off.

"Rachel. Tell me," Zoe demanded, her heart screaming for what could be next.

"He died when he fell off the chair. That was the aneurysm. He was dead. His brain had exploded."

"So..." It all hit Zoe, and her mouth dropped open.

"He was dead when he got back up five hours later. He was dead when he had sex with her," Rachel said.

"Oh, my dear God," Zoe said, her head dropping into her hands.

Chapter Six

The rough-hewn stones of Etienne's dungeon oozed a clammy chill that seeped into Anna's bones. The only light sputtered from a solitary torch, casting grotesque shadows that danced on the walls. She was utterly naked and exposed, chained by her wrists to the cold stone, the weight of her vulnerability a suffocating presence.

Etienne's previously kind eyes gleamed with a feverish intensity as he paced before her within the cell. "Don't you see, Anna? This power, it's a curse. It will destroy you, just like it destroyed those before you."

Though laced with fear, Anna's voice held a tremor of defiance. "It's not a curse, Etienne. It's a part of me, just like it was a part of them." She knew she had a power kindling inside of her. She felt it growing the more suffering she endured hanging by her wrists. Playing the weak victim might throw off Etienne; once her power was strong enough, she could strike. But she couldn't allow him to know her plot. He could read her mind and catch the smallest misstep in her actions, so strong was the spirit. It was a huge advantage for him.

Etienne stopped, his face contorting in a mixture of anger and sorrow. "You don't understand! This power drew the attention of The Dark and brought the local peasants to Luc's doorstep that fateful night. It's what brought me to him that night. I was forced to protect my lord and rid the world of Luc and his hell-spawn."

Etienne's belief that Anna was a witch would be her best defense. "Because they fear what they don't understand," Anna spat. "They fear us." She knew there were more and possibly they could help her. She felt something inside. A warm glow from her heart, not unlike a sisterhood. Perhaps a coven was near and could rescue her if she knew how to call out to them. If only she knew how. But what was The Dark?

Etienne loomed over her, his voice a low growl. "They fear with good reason. This power… it changes you. It twists you." His face softened briefly, a flicker of regret in his eyes. Then the coldness returned, his voice hard. "Whether it's love or obsession, the outcome is the same. The power consumes. It isolates. It…" He faltered, his gaze dropping to the shackles that bound her. "It consumes, just like it did the Mountain Witch. I know she was not always such a foul monster. Everybody begins with innocence in their heart. Faith in God determines the path of good or evil."

Anna's voice dropped to a whisper. "You're afraid of what you don't control, Etienne. You're afraid of me." She knew she could get him riled up and possibly off-balance so she could attack him.

Etienne recoiled as if struck. In the flickering torchlight, the accusation in her eyes was a stark reflection of his growing fear, despite his plan for Anna. The dungeon walls seemed to press in closer, the air thick with a heavy silence. It's what he wanted. It's what he yearned for. Her power was growing. "The power at the chateau, born so long ago in that cellar, I do not know if it lay dormant and you awakened it, or if it was alive and called to you. These things I do not know."

"What power at the chateau? The cellar where Vivienne was entombed?" Anna asked.

He chuckled. "There was something born in the cellar long before Vivienne and long before you took possession of the home." Etienne's voice grew lower and more menacing. "Evil was born there, Anna. Eventually, you will feel it and the entire history will seep into your being, first as a trickle and then as a waterfall—if you are indeed what I believe you are."

Anna felt humiliated being held captive and allowing the specter to taunt her with stories that may or may not be true. Her wet and filthy hair hung before her eyes, but she seethed inside and wished that she could ignite Etienne and finish him.

"Yes. Do it. Unleash flame upon me, witch! Do what your forebears could not and destroy your captor!" he yelled out.

Anna's mind exploded with a vision of a dark-haired woman burning on a pyre while chained to a pole. She felt the flames from her skin so long ago. It was a connection that bound them altogether through time—the coven. There had to be one. She screamed and writhed from the pain of the flames of the past.

Etienne grew ecstatic. "Yes! There it is! Feel what they have passed down to you!" he yelled with raised arms. "Let them fill you with their strength and unleash it!"

Then, at her weakest moment, hanging helpless and naked before the specter of Etienne, Anna felt the charge of electricity in her again. It was like when Luc had attacked her, but it was much stronger this time. It felt good. Her limp body stood upright, and she looked at the shackles on her wrists, concentrating to remove them.

Without warning, Etienne struck her face with a powerful blow from his right fist. Then his left fist hit her. He pounded on her face until blood splattered with each blow.

A low cackling emitted from Anna as her face bled and she stared at her attacker. "More, you little man. Give me more!" The voice was not Anna's. It was low and unearthly. Etienne hit her more. Blood flew through the air. Anna laughed at him in her cackling, throaty new voice. "You hit like a little girl, you weak, pathetic minion of God!" She spat at him, blood squirting from her nose and mouth and clinging to Etienne's face. Then Anna mocked him with a tender, yet chilling, voice. "Can a ghost grow tired, little girl? Are you tired?"

Etienne stepped back as she laughed uproariously at him. He was not looking at Anna any longer. There was something else present inside her. It was working.

Amid her mockery of Etienne, Anna passed out.

Your breath, my dear, is missing
Lush lips I fear not kissing
Eyes so true and sapphire blue
Like a doomed ship, I am listing

Moonlight, a cool caress on white skin, bathed the gardens of Chateau de Mornay in an ethereal glow. Luc, his heart brimming with a joy that eclipsed the formal splendor surrounding him, twirled Anna beneath the star-dusted sky. Like wind chimes in a gentle breeze, her laughter filled the air as she spun back into his arms. Her blonde hair cascaded freely down her back, catching the moonlight like spun gold. In that moment, the world around them faded away. All that remained was the press of her hand in his, the intoxicating scent of lilies that clung to her skirts, and the whispered promise of an ever kindling love.

Luc, ever the poet, spoke first. "Mon amour, you are as radiant as the moon itself tonight."

A blush crept up her cheeks, the rose hue deepening in the moonlight. "Your words are kind, Luc, but surely an exaggeration."

He stopped their dance, holding her gaze with an intensity that sent a delightful shiver down her spine. "Not an exaggeration, a truth. You illuminate this night, just as you illuminate my life."

Anna's eyes, the color of a summer sky, softened. A lifetime of unspoken feelings hung between them, a delicate tapestry woven with stolen glances and secret smiles.

Emboldened by the magic of the moonlit night, Luc took a daring step forward. "Anna," he murmured, his voice husky with emotion, "may I… may I walk you home?"

A hesitant smile touched Anna's lips. "I… I would like that very much, Luc."

As they strolled through the moonlit gardens, arms brushing, a comfortable silence settled between them. It was a silence pregnant with unspoken yearning, a promise whispered on the breath of a summer night. The future stretched before them, uncertain yet filled with a hopeful anticipation, as enchanting as the moonlit gardens they walked through as they walked delicately toward Chateau de Mornay.

Anna awoke and her heart collapsed. She found herself hanging in Etienne's dungeon again. "No!" I want to go back!" she screamed.

Luc's voice resounded in her head. "Mon amour, you're in danger. More danger than you can imagine. I feel it although I can't locate it. Be careful, my love."

Anna opened her eyes again and she was still in the cell. She had briefly stepped back into the dream and heard Luc's chilling warning. Again, she closed her eyes. She was back in the perfect garden.

"Be careful, mon amour," Luc said.

She heard Luc warn her, but his eyes never turned away from the painting he was now working on. Anna climbed up the scaffold that supported Luc, in her usually unladylike way and a long period dress.

"What do you think?" he beamed.

Anna saw the unexpected. The painting was without color, and the chateau was old, gray, and broken, even worse than when she had bought it. The sky in the painting depicted dark clouds and more grayness. It was like the chateau was even older and more destroyed than she had ever seen it. The painting took her heart away to a dreaded place.

"Luc, have you ever heard of The Mountain Witch?" Anna asked.

Without looking away from his work, he replied, "Yes. I grew up with the legend. Every child in this region was frightened by it."

"Do you think the witch is real?" she asked.

"I've never seen a witch, mon amour, so I think not."

Anna reviewed the painting further and noticed that Luc had started to paint cracks in the facade of the chateau.

"Why is it worse?" she asked Luc.

"This is what will happen," he replied, not a shred of personality on his face. "What will happen. That is all."

"If I fail, you mean?"

"It does not matter, mon amour. It is not about gaining nor failing. This will occur. Nothing can stop it."

Chapter Seven

The cabin, a decayed relic of an era long past, lay nestled deep within an ancient forest. It was a place of silence and shadow, where the sunlight faltered before reaching the forest floor. Zoe approached the forsaken abode with a mixture of scholarly curiosity and apprehension. Her purpose was ostensibly academic—to investigate any new information on Eliza Covington. She yearned to know more about the woman she was now convinced was unnatural and indeed a witch. Yet, she was acutely aware that the cabin's grim history lent an air of eerie portent to her mission. Zoe's heart pounded as she approached the old cottage.

She felt that she had reached a crossroads in her studies of Eliza. Yes, it was all academic, but she wanted to see for herself where the old woman had lived and killed. She could continue the paper trail, but Zoe needed to feel the fear and excitement that reading old papers and doctor's notes could not provide. She needed terror. Smelling the same woods and land that Eliza had tread upon could possibly bring her a little closer to the enigmatic woman.

The structure itself stood as a grim testament to its dilapidation. Its walls, possibly once stout and proud, were bowed and splintered, and the roof sagged under the burden of years and neglect. It was where time appeared to have come to a standstill, and the air was thick with the stench of decay and the oppressive weight of forgotten sorrows, and suffering. Zoe felt the evil within the land.

As she examined the area surrounding the cabin, her eyes roved over the ground littered with fallen leaves and underbrush. Despite wearing a thick winter coat, the cold wet air still penetrated and chilled her. The drive had been a long one from Boston, partially through snow, until the weather had changed to cold dampness. She dreaded the drive back in the dark.

Zoe's steps tossed fallen leaves. Then, she noticed something unsettling: beneath the dense mat of leaves lay tiny, white objects partially buried in the dirt. Kneeling to investigate, she found that these objects were teeth—many teeth, scattered in a manner that suggested they had been hastily concealed. Why hadn't the police picked up all the remains? she thought.

Her heart quickened as she pondered the implications of this discovery. The teeth spoke of violence and death, and their presence confirmed the horrific tales of Eliza

Covington's dark rituals. Zoe's scholarly mind struggled to reconcile the empirical with the macabre; here was evidence of the witch's sinister practices, laid bare in the cold light of day. The newspaper articles had told of the cruel tortures and murders perpetrated here, going back to the 1700s.

Compelled by a sense of dread mingled with determination, Zoe continued her search around the cabin. Each turn of the soil and rustle of the leaves seemed to draw her further into the morbid history of the place. Her hands, guided by an uneasy intuition, unearthed more bones—fragments of skeletal remains interred with a disturbing casualness, as though they had been discarded without regard for their former humanity. Again, why were they so easy to find? Why were they not given a proper burial? It was as if the police had dropped the investigation out of lack of interest, perhaps because the remains were so old. Or maybe someone told them to drop it.

As the sun descended, casting long shadows across the ground, her investigation led her to a desolate corner of the cabin's periphery. There, obscured by an accumulation of leaves and dirt, her fingers touched upon a solid, unmistakable object. With mounting urgency, she cleared the debris to reveal a human skull—weathered and fractured, but unmistakably a remnant of a once-living being.

The skull, though partially degraded, bore the telltale marks of violence and neglect. It was a grim testament to the macabre practices that had taken place within the cabin's walls. Zoe's breath caught in her throat as she realized this was another enormous piece of evidence the local authorities had missed—a stark reminder of the horrific deeds that had transpired.

As she held the skull in her hands, the oppressive atmosphere of the forest seemed to close in around her. Realizing that she had unearthed a fragment of a dark past, she shivered with horror and solemnity. The broken cabin, the scattered bones, and the silent witness of the skull combined to create a tableau of unimaginable suffering—a tableau that Zoe had intentionally become a part of.

In the fading daylight, she felt an inescapable sense of connection to the tragic and vicious history of Eliza Covington. Her academic pursuit had led her to confront a reality far darker than she had anticipated, intertwining her fate with the phantasmic echoes of the past. The cabin, with its grim legacy and the remnants of its horrific rituals, had left an indelible mark upon her, a chilling reminder of the depths of human depravity and the inextricable link between past and present. It also confirmed the horror she had witnessed on the videotape, a horror that would never leave her mind. But Zoe had to see it for herself, with her own eyes, the monstrous horror that Eliza had wrought upon this area in Massachusetts for hundreds of years.

Chapter Eight

Rain lashed against the grimy windows of Orrville Sanitarium, the wind howling like a banshee. Inside, fluorescent lights cast a sterile glow on the scene – starkly contrasting the storm raging outside. Eliza lay bound to a metal bed, her once vibrant emerald eyes narrowing coldly. Dr. Roth, a young woman with a nervous tremor in her hands, peered into Eliza's face with a light to see how her eyes responded.

"No signs of any abnormalities, doctor," stammered one of the orderlies, a burly man with sweat beading on his brow despite the room's chill. None of the workers felt safe near Eliza. They had traded tales of strange events in her presence and some orderlies and nurses refused to enter her room, especially since Dr. Howard's death in front of her.

Suddenly, the woman on the metal bed jolted, like she had been shocked by a high voltage. She shook violently, and the two orderlies stepped back, along with Dr. Roth. They watched in terror as the metal bed lifted from the ground with Eliza on it, her body still convulsing madly.

"Oh my God!" Dr. Roth screamed as she watched the five-hundred pound bed levitate like a feather in a breeze.

Eliza's lips, chapped from years of neglect, curved into a humorless smile. "I see you. I see you," she crowed repeatedly in her deep, terrible voice, her eyes distant and focused elsewhere. Years of the sterile purgatory had dimmed the vibrant chaos that was once her magic, but it hadn't extinguished it. Today, it simmered, a hungry beast yearning to be unleashed.

Suddenly, a deafening clap of thunder split the sky, momentarily plunging the room into darkness. As the lights flickered back on, Eliza's eyes blazed with an unnatural emerald light. The metal restraints holding her wrists buckled, and she ripped them free with a snarl. The orderlies reacted instinctively, lunging for her. But it was too late. A surge of raw energy, crackling with the storm's fury outside, erupted from Eliza. The massive bed, with her still on it, flew through the room and crushed one of the orderlies against the wall, his chest caved in grotesquely with a crunch and blood spouting from his mouth, splashing Eliza's face.

Eliza relished the blood on her face and licked at it as she floated off the monstrous bed, the dead orderly hunched over and pouring blood onto the white sheets. "You caged me like a beast," she hissed at Dr. Roth, her voice echoing the storm's power. "Now, you will witness the beast you have unleashed."

The room became a whirlwind of destruction. The fluorescent lights shattered, showering the room in sparks. Heeding her call, the wind howled through the gaping holes she'd ripped in the building, tearing the structure apart.

Huddled in the corner, Dr. Roth watched in horror as Orrville Sanitarium, the symbol of their supposed control, crumbled around them. The sky, a bruised purple and black, was lit by flashes of lightning that illuminated the sanitarium like a macabre stage set. The wind, a constant, shrieking presence, buffeted the building, rattling the windowpanes in their metal frames and sending tremors through the very foundations of the enormous building.

Inside, the patients, already fragile and prone to agitation, grew increasingly restless. Their cries and moans echoed through the long corridors, mingling with the roar of the wind and the shattering of the walls around them. Within moments, their bodies flew high into the blender of destruction, cast free from their oppressors, but shredded to death by Eliza's power. Rain poured into the building, flooding the corridors and turning the floors into treacherous pools. The few remaining patients, driven to the edge of hysteria, roamed the torn halls, their cries mingling with the roar of the storm as they attempted desperately to stay low and avoid getting tossed asunder like tiny dolls.

Eliza stood at the center of the devastation, her eyes blazing with a terrible power. She was a storm goddess reborn from her imprisonment. The wind carried her voice, a chilling prophecy echoing through the ruins. "You sought to control the storm," she bellowed, her voice carried on the howling gale. "But the storm... the storm controls you!"

Eliza focused, picturing the forbidden serpents from the ancient grimoires she'd absorbed in her existence of hundreds of years. A warmth spread through her limbs, then a sickening, exhilarating shift. She screamed, a sound that wasn't quite human, as her arms contorted and stretched. Her skin, usually a pale imitation of its former vibrancy, shimmered and darkened, scales erupting with an unsettling click. Where her hands had been, two sleek, black snakes, with eyes like molten emeralds, now writhed.

Dr. Roth stumbled back, her face contorting in horror and fascination from the metamorphosis before her.

"You think you can confine darkness, Doctor?" Eliza's voice, distorted and guttural, echoed through the room. Her black snake arms hissed in unison, their forked tongues tasting the air, green eyes bright with hunger. The first snake, fueled by years of repressed power, lunged. Its razor-sharp fangs sank deep into the doctor's neck, injecting a potent venom. Roth's eyes widened in silent terror as her grip on life failed, with foam spewing from her mouth, as the venom took immediate hold. The other snake elongated and slithered towards the door, hissing at the remaining orderly. He stumbled back, his face pale with fear. The serpent, a blur of obsidian scales, didn't waste time with theatrics. It struck with lightning speed, impaling the man's chest through his back, the spine breaking and protruding. The man screamed, a high-pitched sound that died abruptly as the huge snake lifted his dying body in the air. It then recoiled and he crumpled to the floor, his eyes wide from witnessing his unearthly killer.

As the storm moved, and broken walls crumbled around her, Eliza turned and faced the fading tumult, now visible from the remains of her room—the only room left even partially intact. With a triumphant laugh, that mingled with the thunder, her arms returned to normal, and she advanced into the heart of the black night, a dark queen reclaiming her throne.

With her arms outstretched, she chanted into the sky. A flash of lightning produced a dark shape, and it plummeted toward her. The cawing of the massive raven announced its presence as its long wings beat hard and allowed for a soft landing on Eliza's shoulder. "Welcome back, my beauty," she hissed as she ran her hand over the raven's head.

As Eliza strolled into the night, the wind howled its approval, a fitting elegy for the fallen Orrville Sanitarium and a chilling promise of the chaos Eliza would unleash upon any obstacles in her way to hold her throne.

Chapter Nine

A tremor ran through the stone floor, dislodging a gout of dust from the cobwebbed rafters above Anna as she hung half awake from her shackled wrists. Then, a shift. The spectral tendrils that anchored her to her existence thinned, and a horrifying clarity washed over her. She was no longer in the familiar dank confines of Etienne's dungeon, but in another damp, torch-lit chamber. The acrid scent of death filled her nostrils. Was it a dream? No, this was something she had never experienced before.

Her vision swam, resolving onto the face of a young woman, no older than twenty-five, strung up by her wrists against a stone wall. Her unbound hair, the color of spun golden wheat, cascaded down her back, stark against the grime that smeared her face. Tears welled in her large, cornflower blue eyes, glistening with a heartbreaking innocence.

Two hulking figures, their faces obscured by shadow, loomed over the young woman. Their guttural voices, laced with sadistic glee, scraped raw against Anna's incorporeal ears.

"Tell us where the others are, doll," one rasped, a cruel glint in his unseen eyes. "It will ease your suffering."

The young woman whimpered, her defiance faltering. "I... I don't know," she choked out, her voice barely a whisper.

A surge of impotent fury pulsed through Anna. She was a helpless spectator, forced to witness this barbarity through the young woman's eyes. Her misty form strained against its tethers, a silent scream building in her chest.

The bruiser on the right, his silhouette a grotesque caricature against the flickering torchlight, produced a wickedly barbed hook similar to one that holds large meat slabs. A whimper escaped the young woman's lips as he drew it closer, the metal glinting malevolently.

Anna, a powerless wraith tethered to the scene's periphery, recoiled. A primal sense of dread filled her, a chilling echo of her torture at the hands of Etienne. Yet, this torture felt different. It wasn't the detached observation of a ghost, but a visceral, horrifying empathy, as if the young woman's terror resonated within Anna's phantom form.

"We have ways of making you talk, girl," the brute rasped, his voice a gravelly caress of menace. We need to find all of your scum." The torchlight danced across the cruel amusement, twisting his features, as the hook drew nearer.

The young woman flinched, her gaze darting between the men, searching for a flicker of mercy in their shadowed faces. Finding none, she squeezed her eyes shut, her breath catching in a sob.

A desperate plea tore from Anna's core, a soundless scream that died unheard in the cold stone chamber. The shadowy ropes that bound her to her existence strained, a silent, agonizing resistance against her forced captivity.

Suddenly, the sound of a key scraping against the rusted lock of the cellar door pierced the tense silence. The two men exchanged glances, and a flicker of unease crossed their brutish features.

The heavy oak door of the cellar groaned open, revealing a cloaked figure standing in the shaft of moonlight that spilled through the entrance. The figure, tall and gaunt, its face obscured by the hood's shadow, surveyed the scene with an unnerving stillness. "Leave us," the figure commanded, its voice a low murmur that sent shivers down Anna's spine.

The two brutes hesitated momentarily, their bravado faltering under the figure's unwavering gaze. Then, with muttered curses, they retreated through the doorway, leaving the young woman limp against the wall.

The figure strode towards her, its movements deliberate and measured. As it drew closer, the moonlight filtering through the cellar door illuminated a face etched with deep lines and haunted by myriad unspoken sorrows. It was an older woman in her forties, her eyes, an unsettling shade of green, held a spark of compassion and something far more ancient and unsettling. Her hair was dark, a vacant black unlike anything Anna had seen.

Upon getting a better glimpse of the mysterious older woman, Anna couldn't escape the thought that the woman looked like her in about ten years. It couldn't be, she thought, but Anna was powerless to do anything except remain a prisoner within the young woman's vision. She longed to keep the older woman in view so she could get a better look. Alas, she was foiled.

With surprising gentleness, the older woman untied the young woman's binds. She slumped to the floor, gasping for breath, her body racked with tremors. The older woman knelt beside her, her touch surprisingly warm on the young woman's chilled skin.

"You are safe now, child," the older woman murmured, her voice a soothing balm against the terror. "They cannot harm you any longer."

The young woman looked up at the older woman, her eyes wide and filled with gratitude and dawning fear. "Who are you?" she whispered, her voice hoarse.

A flicker of a smile, tinged with sadness, touched the woman's lips. "A friend," she replied enigmatically. "A friend who knows your plight."

As the older woman spoke, Anna felt a shift in the preternatural tethers that bound her. A tendril of connection, faint but undeniable, reached out from the older woman towards the young woman. A jolt of energy surged through Anna, a terrifying and exhilarating connection. Was this...what true power felt like? Was this a message for her or a warning? Why was she forced into the vision and feelings of this young woman from another time? Who was she? Who was this savior that resembled Anna?

Just as it began, the vision ended. The tether was gone, and Anna returned to her corporeal form, hanging naked from her shackles.

Without warning, the energy surged within her again. The power, the zeal, like a drug that never fades, blasted through Anna. It made her drunk and carefree. She never wanted it to end. When she reveled in her newfound power, she felt an intoxicating rush coursing through her veins, like a heady blend of adrenaline and exhilaration. The world around her faded into the background as she savored the thrill of control, her thoughts sharp and clear, yet tinged with a reckless edge. In those moments, she felt freedom that made her believe she could bend reality to her will. But beneath the exhilaration lurked a flicker of unease, a whispered reminder that such intoxicating heights often came with perilous falls.

A mist then appeared in front of her and out stepped Etienne. He stopped before her, his eyes squinting at Anna's wounded face from his repeated beatings. "What happened? I felt something horrid just now," he said, looking her naked body up and down, surprisingly aroused by the way she was admiring him.

Anna appeared drunk and her eyes were not her own. Gone were the beautiful blue gemstones, replaced by two hauntingly bright green eyes.

She leaned forward until her face was mere inches from his. "You know how much I've lost because I followed my principles? Because I was the good girl? Maybe it's time for me to be bad, Etienne. Maybe that's what I want," she said as she writhed before her captor, her blood caked in her hair and down her breasts and abdomen.

Suddenly, her shackles opened and she was free with a few clicks of metal. But Etienne had not done it. Anna was upon him before he could flinch. However, she didn't try to kill him. Quite the opposite. Her mouth landed on his, her tongue deep inside. She reached down to his bulge and squeezed it just enough for him to know how seriously she wanted him. Her grasp made him engorged. And engorged it was. She felt his whole nine inches of hardness through the thin fabric of his breeches. She aggressively reached inside and pulled it out. Her whole hand didn't come close to wrapping completely around it. She knelt and opened her wet mouth and took him in. His girth stretched her lips as she sucked and bobbed her head. He grabbed her head with both hands and forced it into her mouth, his balls knocking her chin. At first slowly but then faster and harder. Her nose smashed his abdomen as he forced his size between her dry lips.

  Anna felt the pressure on the back of her throat and gagged a little before remembering how to handle a large cock. She made her adjustments and let it slide down her throat. Etienne moaned as she expertly navigated his size. After a moment or two of bliss, Etienne picked up Anna by the head and thrust her against the cell bars. He lifted her naked body by her tight ass and pushed it against the bars. He felt her holes and wetness as his fingers went for a grip under her thighs. He felt her fur and rubbed her wet lips. Anna's legs spread open, Etienne let his large cock slide slowly into her perfection. Their mouths were already entangled in passionate heat, and Anna let out a groan of pain as his size began thrusting. His kiss muffled the sound as she screamed into his lungs. He lifted her up and down forcefully on his cock, her legs spread as far as she could to take his size.

Etienne pushed her up a little, and her breasts fell into his mouth, where he sucked and licked furiously at the beautiful young, yet changed and disheveled Anna. He enjoyed the sweet sweat beading down her neck and licked at it as he bit her. She smelled foul after her captivity, but it drove his passion even higher. It reminded him of bedding women back in his own time, the last time he had been with a woman.

Part of what made it so good for Etienne was that he knew Luc was watching. Somewhere, somehow Luc was watching his old friend giving Anna the best fuck she had possibly ever had, judging by her screams of passion. It made Etienne grin, but he truly did feel for Anna. He wanted her to be his as much as possible. He wanted what she had to offer.

Anna screamed as she orgasmed multiple times against the bars. "Fuck me! Fuck me harder!" she yelled into Etienne's mouth as she kissed him deeper.

Etienne slammed her quicker until he orgasmed and groaned like a raging animal. Their breathing slowed as he pulled out, his semen dripping from Anna's sore lips. He lowered her until she stood before him. Etienne examined Anna's wrists, which were bruised, but what caught his attention more was that the shackles were gone. She had freed herself. Anna had done what he knew she was capable of.

"Come upstairs with me," he said as he held her hand and led her out of the cell.

Chapter Ten

A chilling wind through chambers bare,
The heart grows still, a frozen prayer,
And silence claims the soul's despair

The dense woods near the ruins of Orrville Sanitarium, shrouded in perpetual twilight, seemed to recoil from Eliza's approach. Her raspy, pained groan, a sound like wind whistling through a crypt, echoed off the ancient trees, their skeletal branches clawing at the bruised underbelly of the clouds. Unlike the heroines of lore, Eliza was a creature of the night, her beauty long ravaged by time and dark pacts. Yet, in her wild, untamed mane and eyes that burned with an unnatural green light, a power sent shivers down unseen, distant spines.

With a muttered incantation, and a gnarled hand that sketched arcane symbols in the air, Eliza summoned her domain. The fetid earth seemed to writhe in response, and a wooden cabin materialized through the oppressive darkness. It rose from the woods like a specter, its skeletal frame straining under the weight of a moss-ridden roof. Dark windows gaped like empty sockets, blind eyes staring into the gloom.

This was Eliza's sanctuary, where the shadows cowered at her command. Stepping inside, she was met by a familiar wave of dark power, a grim satisfaction twisting her lips. Here, amidst the shadows and whispers of the woods, she would weave her spells, a predator in her lair, waiting for the next unsuspecting soul to stumble into her web.

Later that night, past the witching hour, a scythe moon leered through a skeletal canopy, casting the gnarled trees of the woods into monstrous silhouettes. Eliza, her black cloak billowing behind her like a raven's wing, navigated the treacherous terrain with practiced ease. More incantations followed as she held out her right hand. With a quick, brilliant flash of light, moonlight glinted off the silver skeleton key nestled in her palm, connected to a leather necklace she had also summoned. The key was a stark reminder of her father and where she had come from. Home. Where she was born. She carefully put the necklace over her head with great respect.

Tonight, the air crackled with an unnatural energy. Eliza's suspicions, a gnawing unease in the pit of her stomach, had intensified into a howling certainty. Something foreign, something out of place, had trespassed upon the ancient magic that clung to these woods like a shroud.

As she crested a hillock in search of the unease, the sound of frantic rustling cut through the lonely silence. A young woman lay sprawled at the base of a particularly gnarled oak. Not a villager, Eliza recognized the foreign, mass-produced garb that clung to her trembling form. A city-dweller lost and terrified.

The woman, barely more than a girl, struggled to her knees, her eyes wide with terror. "Please," she whimpered, her voice ragged. "Help me. I'm lost. I don't know how I got here. I was just at a party and…"

Eliza approached cautiously, the girl's outlandish attire fueling her apprehension. This creature was an anomaly in Eliza's world, with her strange, smooth skin and bewilderment as palpable as the damp earth beneath their feet. "Who are you, child? How did you come to be here?" Eliza's voice, roughened by centuries spent whispering incantations to the wind, starkly contrasted the girl's panicked pleas.

"I... I don't know," the girl stammered. "One minute I was at a stupid party, the next... this." She gestured wildly at the looming trees. "I have no service on my phone!"

A phone? Service? Eliza frowned, the words as foreign to her ears as the girl's appearance. This creature, so utterly reliant on unseen forces, sent an excited shiver down her spine. Yet, a flicker of something resembling pity stirred within her. "Stay put, child," Eliza rasped. "I shall find my way back to the village and send help."

The girl's eyes, however, darted nervously around the clearing. "No! Please, don't leave me alone." Laced with a strange desperation, her voice sent a cold tremor through Eliza.

A sudden gust of wind howled through the trees, extinguishing the moon and plunging the clearing into an inky blackness. The girl screamed a sound that ripped through the unnatural stillness.

In that suffocating darkness, Eliza's premonition solidified into a chilling certainty. This creature, lost and afraid, was not what it seemed. It was a conduit, a vulnerability in the veil that separated her world from something far more sinister. A horrifying transformation began. Black veins pulsed beneath Eliza's pale skin, spreading like a spiderweb. She let out a feral shriek, and the frightened young girl fell back at the shocking noise. Eliza's fingers elongated with a sickening crack, splitting and twisting into gnarled, black branches. Long and wickedly sharp thorns erupted from their tips, dripping with an inky ichor. The metamorphosis continued, her arms becoming twisted boughs.

The young girl's following scream was a symphony of terror that comforted Eliza. It clawed at the darkness, a grotesque melody that echoed through the woods long after it had ceased.

When the moon finally reclaimed its dominion over the clearing, revealing the girl crumpled and bloody like a discarded doll tossed into a briar patch, a cold satisfaction settled over Eliza. The trespasser was gone, the veil repaired. The woods held their secrets safe, for now.

As Eliza turned to leave, the branches of her fingers returned to her normal form, a grim testament to the unnatural horror she had just executed. The world outside might have changed, but the old ways of protection and retribution remained vigilant.

Unseen forces had gifted her fuel in the form of the teenage girl, and for that she was thankful. Like a spider taking its poisoned prey into its home, Eliza dragged the girl's contorted body to her newly spawned cabin. Within it, she would proceed to mutilate the body, separating hair, eyes, and fingers to regain more power that she had lost while in captivity at the sanitarium. Eliza knew she would need the power for what was to come. There was another.

Chapter Eleven

"I told you about the mountain witch earlier," Etienne said as he sprawled out on a fur rug before a giant fireplace that sent an orange glow across the dark room, Anna's naked body wrapped around his. They coiled together like an albino python squeezing its prey. Etienne continued, "I fear, and am somehow delighted, that you are becoming something akin to her. As I said."

"Why would you be delighted?" Anna asked, her naked body writhing and green eyes set aflame by the fire light.

"Because your power is something I want," he said.

"You sound exactly like Luc, but he didn't have the nerve to tell me so bluntly. He hid it behind lies," Anna replied.

"Yes, he did. I'm glad you understand his selfish designs for you and Vivienne Laurent. He was taking the good from you and her. Sucking it from your being and sending you on your way down the beginning of the dark road."

Anna rolled on top of Etienne, straddling his crotch and feeling his penis begin to swell on her thigh. "If Luc stole my good heart, what are you taking from me?" she asked as she leaned forward, her face an inch from the corporeal specter beneath her.

"I have no interest in your good nature, Anna. What I want is The Dark within you. Whereas Luc harnessed love to selfishly steal your fledgling power, I will employ pain to hone it and bind it to you forever. The Dark will prevail within you, witch."

Anna smiled unlike she ever had before, her face contorted and eyes squinting with pure evil. The promise of power intoxicated her. Hunger boiled in her green eyes as she licked Etienne's tongue. She felt his arousal and reached behind her, grasping his hardness and pushing it inside her waiting lips. It slid in easier this time. Anna was in control, and she rocked slowly on top of him so that the wet sheen of his cock was visible from behind them. His girth stretched her labia further than she had ever felt during sex. Normally she wouldn't enjoy the pain, but the new Anna reveled in the pleasure, with a tinge of intense throbbing that added to her arousal.

Then, in a surprise to Etienne, a man from another time and surely unfamiliar with the position, Anna slid up and sat on his mouth. His eyes went wide and a maniacal smile presented itself before being buried in her spread wet pinkness. Anna grinded on him slowly as Etienne moaned feverishly. He reached down and stroked his wet cock as she pushed harder to get his tongue deeper inside her. Anna's hips sped up as she approached orgasm. She then felt hot semen hit her back as Etienne came like a fountain, his moans contained within her wet pink lips. His vocal vibrations intensified her pleasure as Anna rode his face faster, leaning back to get a drop of semen on her finger. She sucked on it as she orgasmed hard and loudly.

Covered in sweat from the sex and heat of the fire, she collapsed on the fur rug next to him, her green eyes dimming as her breathing slowed. Her eyes met his. "What am I doing?" she asked, frustrated and feeling her old self for a moment.

"You are in the midst of changing. The Anna you were yesterday is gone forever. Eventually you will not recognize yourself," Etienne said with a cocksure grin.

Her breathing increasing, Anna protested, "This isn't what I want! I can't be here. This isn't happening! Take me back to my old life!" In panic, she tried to pull herself up, but Etienne waved his hand, and she fell asleep gently on the fur rug, warmed by the fire and safely under his protection.

Chapter Twelve

I awoke this day without you
The world empty but of sorrow
I dreamed a dream so golden
And yearned for a sweet tomorrow

Anna found herself dreaming again of Chateau de Mornay, except this time she was in bed with Luc in the great bedroom, his father's room in his time. The room was golden and had gilded sparkles floating in the fresh air. The fresco ceiling, with Lazarus, as beautiful as its first drying paint. Anna breathed it in and sighed. She was happy. It was a new sensation to her. Joy, elation, like when she had married Brad. But the feeling was for Luc now. The thought of Brad disappeared instantly when Anna rolled over and her eyes met Luc's, bluer than ever before, blue amidst the golden room, like gems glowing on a beautiful amulet. They lay naked and it was bliss. "I don't want to go back," she whispered as if prying ears were present. "Don't make me leave you again."

"Mon amour, that is not my doing. When you go, so do I. I want to stay here the same as you. I implore you not to leave me," Luc whispered, his warm breath sending chills down Anna's neck.

"Then I won't," Anna replied. She kissed his lush lips, tiny golden sparkles landing between their skin and giving a minuscule electric shock that made her heart flutter like butterflies. It felt so right.

Regardless of the power of her dream, she awoke alone on the fur animal rug before the nearly dead fire. She was still naked. It had been another dream with Luc. Was it only a dream, or was Luc in another plane, waiting for her?

Anna looked over at the wall. A small amount of light beamed through a single window high in the main room. It was day, but inside Marchessault Castle, it was always night.

She pulled herself up, her green eyes returned to blue, and walked over to a wall adorned with several tapestries and weapons. She was amazed at the collection, but at the same time, an urge overpowered her. Her head pounded furiously as she reached up and grasped a gladiator sword.

Suddenly a mist appeared before her and Etienne stepped out frantically. "Anna, don't!" he yelled. "Stop!"

"I want to be with you forever, Luc," Anna said as she plunged the sword up through her torso and into her heart.

PART TWO

Chapter Thirteen

Corveau, France, 1685

A young woman watched with haunting, crystal blue eyes from the doorway to her father's patisserie as two soldiers hammered a mandate from the king onto a post across the cobblestone street. Her beauty had no rival, and her perfectly smooth face made her look even younger than her twenty-three years. Hair of golden wheat with tinges of red, (more red when seen in the afternoon sun) that curled down to her waist, wonderfully outlined her porcelain-like face. Although she was not a peasant, due to her father's popular baker vocation in Corveau, she preferred to wear bland colors and clothes because it made her feel closer to God. She believed he preferred a more timid woman in clothing and behavior. Her Calvinist upbringing had taught the young woman that she would secure a place of salvation with God if she led a proper life.

She was a Huguenot, and her father was one of the highest ranking Protestants in Corveau. Due to the fragile state of religion in their country at the time, the Huguenots were the Protestant minority and easy targets for bullying, intimidation, and sometimes murder by the majority Roman Catholics. This was why the young woman always kept her eyes observant. She knew they were being hunted. Hunted because they were Protestant and fighting the status quo of Catholicism. Hunted because they were brave and believed in a different path to God.

A crowd gathered around the paper mandate as soon as the soldiers moved to the next street to begin hammering again. A bevy of sighs, groans, and gasps emanated as each villager read the proclamation:

By his grace, King Louis XIV, hereby revokes the Edict of Nantes and therefore Protestant heresy is presumed as high treason against God and mankind. It will be dealt with swiftly by punishments of torture, loss of property, public humiliation, and death.

Several villagers walked away briskly with their hands covering their mouths so as not to let their emotions elicit suspicion. A few sobbed, unable to contain their feelings about their country's fall from tolerance that the edict of Nantes had granted all citizens nearly one-hundred years prior by King Henry IV.

The young woman needed to see what the commotion was all about. She watched carefully while going down the stone road, always aware of prying eyes and spies for the extraordinarily pious king. Reaching the crowd, she waited until her turn came so that she retained her politeness while others rudely pushed their way forward to the paper. Finally, she reached it and her face went whiter than ever before in her young life. Her heart skipped and fear struck her like a lashing to her bare back. She knew what was to come and gathered her dress to walk faster back to her father's patisserie. Upon reaching the door, she pushed it open, entered, and closed it quickly. She pulled the lock on the door and laid her forehead on the glass, looking to see if anyone had trailed her.

"What is it, my sweet tart?" a booming voice from behind her asked. Her father, Francois Lourvois, was a broad-chested man in his forties, tall and handsome with graying hair pulled back in a satin tie.

"The king has issued an edict that officially makes us enemies of the state, papa!" the young woman replied in French, tears ending in her eyes.

"What do you mean?" he asked.

She began sobbing. "It goes even further than what they do now with soldiers living in our friends' homes and harassing them. We can be hurt, papa! They can burn our churches and torture us into converting. It's not about bullying anymore! They can take your bakery! They can take our home! We have to go!"

Francois rushed from behind the counter and embraced his only daughter. "There, there, my sweet. God will protect us because we honor him at all times." He pushed her back enough to look into her flawless blue eyes, now beginning to show capillaries in her white corneas from the tears. "I will seek out my friends and meet about this at once. Stay inside with the door locked and the curtains pulled. Please."

He gathered his brown and worn Justaucorps knee-length coat and threw it on over his white shirt, which he often wore while making pastries and bread in the patisserie. Francois kissed his daughter on the forehead and then rushed out the door.

The young woman locked it behind him and frantically pulled the lace curtains shut as tears streamed down her face. She knew it was hopeless if they came to take the family patisserie. Soldiers would break the door and force themselves in. She had watched the dragoon soldiers, billeted in her friends' homes, push them down and beat them to get them to leave France for their religious beliefs. It had happened for many years. She had grown to despise her own country's army because of their horrid behavior toward French citizens. Friends had fled, some were forced to convert, and even some had disappeared with rumors going around the village of executions. Executions just for respecting God more properly! It infuriated and sickened her.

She felt like vomiting due to the intense fear inside her. The young woman had never been more frightened. She felt like a caged animal being locked in the patisserie. She dared not venture out into the street for fear of being abducted.

Hurried footsteps pounded on the stones outside as some villagers ran from the simple piece of paper that held such power. She watched them fly by the window in the growing fear outside. The wooden sign for Le Corveau Inn across the street hung loose on its chains and shimmied slightly from everyone running by. Surely more soldiers would enter the village, flushing out all the Huguenots toward whatever fate God had for them. Her cries became louder as she heard distant musket shots. Were they warning shots, or were people being gunned down? Each shot made her wince. She wished she could be anywhere else but trapped in her family's patisserie in Corveau. How would they hide? Would they flee France now that their lives and livelihood were in danger?

    The young woman wished she had her mother to comfort her. She wanted to bury her face into her chest like she had always done as a child when she had needed her mother's sweet grace. But her mother Helene was gone. She had died suddenly two years prior from what the doctor's termed an aneurysm of the brain. The disorder was new to the doctors. The young woman saw her that morning and by night her mother was dead. Francois had found her lying on the floor of their bedroom. It had happened while she was dressing. The autopsy confirmed that a vessel in her brain had ruptured, killing her instantly. It was the only saving grace for the young woman. At least her beloved mother did not suffer. She couldn't imagine suffering in pain. It made her feel ill again, so she decided to take deep breaths and think of her mother; the way she smelled like flowers and her voice's soothing cadence.

    The young woman felt the safest hiding place was behind the counter. Maybe if soldiers broke in, they would see the patisserie empty and move on. She sat down and leaned against the counter, pulling her knees closer and making herself as small as a mouse. They would never find her here.

Nightfall came and the young woman's father was still gone. Maybe he had found his friends, and they were meeting in a basement somewhere? Perhaps they were planning to flee the village and head to Spain, just over the Pyrenees mountains to their west? She had to keep her thoughts on the positive because dread was on the verge of taking over. She was hungry as she continued to lean against the counter, fearing every sound coming from the street. The musket shots continued, and she now knew they weren't warning shots any longer. She was certain that death had come to Corveau from just one piece of paper.

Every footstep she heard outside made her shiver. However, the chances of someone stopping were slim. The young woman knew that there were bigger Huguenot targets in the village. The church would be a likely place to ransack first. The soldiers knew that destroying their church would kill the Protestants' will quickly, and they would then be more likely to flee.

The door rattled. She hadn't even heard anyone approaching. It rattled again, harder this time. She had nowhere to go if the soldiers entered. She would be taken away and possibly shot or hanged; or even worse, tortured to repent or convert. The young woman's pulse accelerated, and she could feel it in her temples. She feared an aneurysm like her mother had died from. Or maybe it was a better way to go than whatever fate could be coming her way?

The rattling stopped, and she took a deep breath. That's when the glass broke. She gasped. Was it a stone to vandalize or was someone trying to break in? The young woman closed her eyes and prayed hard for her father to return and save her. She pictured him rushing the soldiers with his huge body and killing them swiftly with a sword.

She heard the lock click. The door swung open with a slight creak. The young woman wished she was smaller and could crawl into a mouse hole and stay there forever. She didn't hear footsteps, but rather the dragging of feet. They were the quietest soldiers she'd ever heard. The dragging feet came closer and closer. They were just on the other side of the counter. Silence. Then breathing. The whistle of air through a nose.

Glass shattered just over her head. They had smashed the display of pastries at the counter. The young woman then heard chewing as she dared not even breathe. The soldiers were stealing her father's pastries.

The dragging foot slid across the floor and was almost on her side of the counter. She closed her eyes as tears squeezed out and ran silently down her cheeks. It was so quiet that the young woman heard the tears fall from her chin and hit the top of her dress. Drip, drip. She knew they had spotted her, but she didn't want to see them. Maybe if she kept her eyes shut, God would make her invisible. Yes.

The young woman smelled them before she saw them. They stunk like beggars or even some vile animal ravaging trash. The dragging footsteps approached her—a step, then a slide, a step, then a slide—over and over. It stopped only inches from her. She knew the soldier was there.

He knelt, and she felt his breath on her face. "What's your name, doll?" he whispered in a deep, condescending tone.

The young woman kept her wet eyes shut and ignored him. Maybe he would go away if she didn't speak?

"I asked you what your name is," he whispered again, this time close to her temple so she felt the tickle of his disgusting breath inside her ear. He stunk so bad that she was about to vomit.

She prayed for an aneurysm. "Please, God, take me from here," she thought repeatedly.

"Look at me, doll," he whispered again as he stood back up, towering over her, judging by his high voice.

The young woman decided to open her eyes. She had no choice. She turned her head up toward him and blinked several times. Her eyes were so wet that it was a blur.

Then she saw him.

He wasn't a soldier. He was an ugly man with thinning long hair and an angular face. A manic smile filled his countenance as she saw him. His teeth were rotted and some were missing.

"There you go, doll. See? That wasn't hard, now was it?" The man's slow, deep voice was a little louder than the gentle whisper from before. He was indeed very tall. His left leg was deformed, and he had a frightening lean. He licked his lips with a sickening hunger in his strained eyes.

Then the young woman screamed.

105

She was pulled out of the patisserie and into the street while screaming, but nobody helped her. Chaos had overtaken Corveau and the villagers, if they intervened, would become targets of the militant Catholics as well, despite their affiliation.

With the dragging foot, the deformed man pulled the young woman to a horse and cart. Another ugly man, much younger than his accomplice, was seated on the cart with the single horse's reigns in his hands.

The young woman was easily heaved into the cart by the deformed monster, praying the entire time that her father would come to her rescue. Where was he? She had to keep praying as hard as she could. It kept her focused and put the terror of being abducted away for the time being.

They both sat behind the driver as the cart entered the cobblestone streets. They didn't need to move quickly. The king's official edict gave them power to defend their actions, and nobody in their right minds would intervene. The young woman watched as mostly soldiers led away many other Huguenots, but also fellow citizens - Catholics who had decided to judge their fellow man and undo a hundred years of religious tolerance within France.

Eventually the cart left Corveau and entered the main dirt road out of the village. "You are a brave one, doll," the deformed man with disgusting teeth said to her. "We'll see how you hold up when we take you home."

Home? Where was that?, the young woman thought. Her heart raced as she realized that her papa wouldn't be saving her, and all the prayers she had done were for nothing.

After a ten minute ride from hell, the cart turned and stopped at a new wrought iron gate with a stone wall and ivy. The driver hopped out and opened the gate before returning to the cart, prompting the horse, and continuing up the stone path.

The young woman recognized where they were going. The four-year-old Chateau de Mornay loomed in the distance and her heart sank. She had watched the construction since she was a girl. The de Mornay family were mysterious and kept to themselves. They were wealthy, but not aristocracy. She didn't know where their wealth came from. At this point she didn't care. She knew they weren't taking her to have tea. The young woman's body trembled as they approached the hulking white beast of a building. She had never seen a chateau in her young life, or anything even close to the size and beauty that her eyes were witnessing. Its outer serenity belied what awaited her inside. Punishment was coming. She knew it.

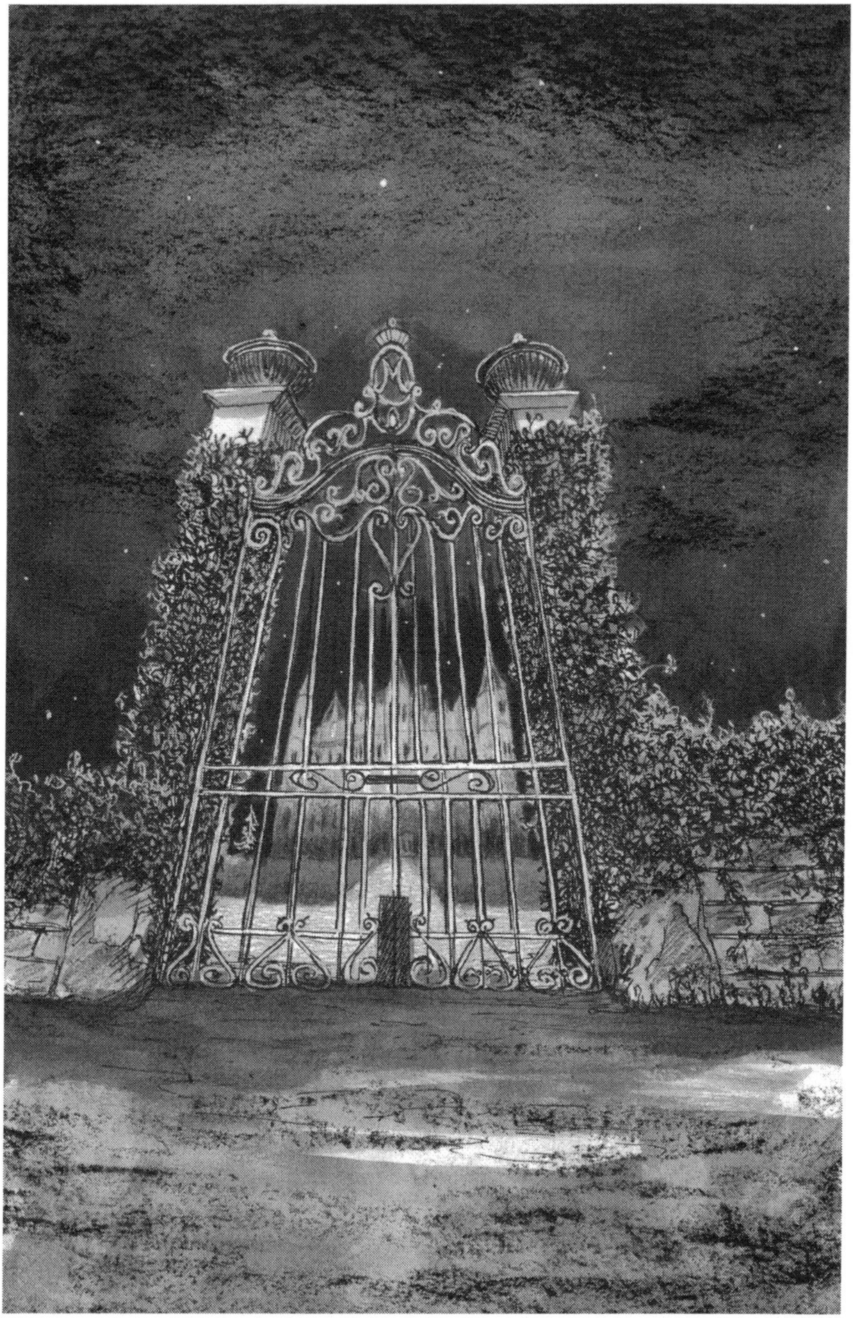

Chapter Fourteen

The young woman's vision swam, the stone floor of Chateau de Mornay's cellar tilting beneath her as she awoke. It was the next day, or at least that's how she felt based on the hunger in her stomach. Her unbound hair, usually a crown of golden curls, clung damply to her neck, the coppery tang of blood thick in her nostrils.

The two burly men, their faces contorted with a mix of piety and sadistic glee, loomed over her. Their leader with the limp foot spat on the ground beside her. "Heretic! Renounce your ways, embrace the Lord's light, or face his wrath!" His voice boomed, echoing off the rough-hewn stones.

The young woman choked back a sob. Easy for him to speak of light, surrounded by flickering torches that cast grotesque shadows on the walls. Her years had been spent renouncing Satan and living a pious, God serving life. To deny it was to deny herself.

The other man, a younger brute, circled her like a vulture. His calloused hand snatched a stray curl, twisting it cruelly. "Speak, bitch! Perhaps a taste of God's punishment will loosen your impudent tongue."

Pain flared as he yanked her head back, his grip leaving a burning mark on her scalp. Tears welled in her eyes, blurring the scene further. She wouldn't give them the satisfaction. She wouldn't break.

The old, deformed brute, impatiently twisting his features, grabbed a thick metal handled mace from a nearby stand. Its surface, polished to a cruel sheen, reflected the flickering flames. "Let us see if your resolve withstands this, demon-spawn."

The young woman flinched, the weight of the weapon a terrible promise. Its heavy, spiked top could cave in her head with one blow. But before he could bring it down, a bloodcurdling woman's scream tore through the dungeon. It wasn't hers.

The men froze, their gazes darting toward the iron bars that separated the main dungeon from a smaller torture chamber. A sickening wet thud echoed from within, followed by a strangled gurgle.

The deformed brute cursed under his breath. "That fool, Dubois! Didn't I tell him to make the questioning quieter?"

His accomplice grunted in agreement, his hand loosening on the young woman's hair. The unexpected reprieve sent a jolt of relief through her, a fragile hope flickering amidst the despair.

"We'll deal with you later, Huguenot," the deformed one snarled, shoving her roughly against the wall. He and Jean hurried towards the chamber, the heavy clang of the iron door slamming shut behind them.

Alone in the sudden silence, the young woman sagged against the cold stone. Her body ached, but it was the cold dread that settled deep within her that was most terrifying. What awaited her when they returned, their sadistic fervor likely amplified by the interruption?

A single tear traced a cold path down her cheek as the minutes stretched into an eternity. Maybe they were right. Maybe she should confess to something, anything, to make the pain stop. But the thought of denying her God, the very essence of her soul, was unbearable. All of this just because she was Protestant.

With a shaky breath, the young woman pushed herself upright. She wouldn't give them the satisfaction of seeing her fear. She would endure. She had to. There had to be a way out of this, a way to escape the clutches of her captors' cruelty. Even in the dimmest corner of the dungeon, a spark of defiance flickered within her, refusing to be extinguished.

"Go get the pear," the man with the dragging foot said loudly to his colleague from the other chamber. The young woman wondered what the pear was. She looked around in the torch light and noticed a veritable array of unusual machines and devices. Some had hooks, some had ropes, but most of them had spikes. There was a wooden chair with the arms and seat covered in pointed, dirty black spikes. Next to it, was a wooden slab with gears and rope. The young woman had never seen anything like the machines. The torch light flickered more, and she noticed pools of black blood on the stone floor near the machines. There were also body parts and a legless torso and head hanging from a meat hook and chain. Her heart raced, and she couldn't hold back a strong bout of sobs. She was certain that her young life would end here. Screams of intense pain erupted from the unseen chamber where the two brutes had gone. The young woman heard a metallic cranking sound and a man's voice pleaded for them to stop.

"Renounce your ways and the pain will cease," the deformed man's voice said with a coy playfulness.

Silence greeted him followed by cries of, "no, no, no!" as the metallic cranking continued. The man screamed louder as the unseen device did its work.

The young woman had to stop thinking about what they were using on him. A pear? She had to hang onto any last bit of innocence before her time came. "Blessed be thy God, protector from evil. Hasten me from here, oh God," the young woman whimpered as the man's roars of pain suddenly stopped in the other chamber. She heard rustling and saw them dragging the man by her cell door.

Despite his face being covered in wounds and blood, the young woman saw that it was her father Francois. "Papa! No!" she called out. His baker's white shirt was brown and red with dirt and blood. The two torturers glanced at her and smiled.

"Don't worry, doll, Papa will wake up soon and you can chat with him about renouncing your family's evil ways," the deformed brute said with a hiss.

They lifted Francois's limp body onto the wooden slab with the crank and ropes. They tied the ropes to his feet and outstretched hands over his head.

"The rack will soften his tongue when he wakes," the other brute spat.

A further cry of pain erupted from the other chamber. This time it was another girl. The young woman could only put her hands over her ears to staunch the hellish sounds of Chateau de Mornay's cellar.

Only known to the young woman as gossip and rumors, the cellar was the region's primary location for forced confessions through torture. The three de Mornay men were demented souls who collected medieval torture devices with their riches and used them to great effect to keep the Protestant population to a minimum. They had the blessing of the king to carry out God's will to convert Protestants and destroy witches, if they found any.

"Papa?" the young woman whispered to her father as he began to stir on the rack.

The two brutes had moved into the other chamber amidst screams and grunts, as they had their way with the poor young soul whose life was surely near its end too.

Francois turned his head slowly. "Elizabeth?"

"Yes, Papa!"

"No. Please tell me you're not here. Please tell me you're safe and I hear a siren's call," he said amidst his sobs.

"Papa, it's me. They found me hiding in the shop," Elizabeth said while crying. Her heart hurt for her father, who would rather not even be near her at this moment.

"You need to find a way out of here. Do you hear me, Elizabeth? I've seen things here that nobody should ever witness. I won't allow them to get to you. I'll do everything I…" Francois's voice trailed off as he realized he was bound tightly and there was no physical way for him to rescue his daughter. He knew he was doomed, but God had to at least save Elizabeth. "Oh God, my almighty savior, send my daughter far from here. Save her and allow me to suffer for the both of us."

Elizabeth tried to hear her father's prayers over the assault occurring in the chamber next door. She couldn't drown out the young girl's screams as the men took turns rhythmically grunting in their sick ways.

Francois called out louder. "Elizabeth! Don't allow them to take you! You must pray and then find a way to end your own life. There must be something in your cell. You don't want to live through what they'll do to you. Please, daughter!"

Looking frantically around her cell, Elizabeth only saw a small pile of hay. But there were stones in the wall and the floor. She could crush her head...

She rushed back to the door and looked through the bars as she heard the brutes returning. They dragged an unconscious, naked teenage girl by one arm as they passed her cell. Elizabeth put her hand to her mouth to contain the scream. The girl was probably still alive, but barely, and she had wounds everywhere on her body. What else could they do to her?

Then she heard her father's voice call out. "If I renounce my ways and convert, will you spare my daughter?"

The two torturers looked at each other and then the girl on the ground. The deformed one said, "looks like it's too late for your daughter, Huguenot." The two men chuckled cruelly.

"My daughter is in the cell. She is innocent and young and has her whole life before her. Let her go and do what you will with me. I'll even confess," Francois said desperately, blood seeping from his mouth from broken teeth.

"I rather like that idea. Don't you, Pierre?" The deformed brute said to the lesser torturer.

"Sounds fine to me, Jean."

Elizabeth watched as they hefted the unconscious girl onto the spiked chair. Instantly she awoke and screamed in massive pain as the spikes drove into her legs and buttocks. Jean shackled her arms into the spiked arm rests of the chair and pushed down hard. The poor girl screamed even louder. The spikes entered her forearms as she tried to raise her body.

"Here, hold this," Pierre said as he dropped a large rock into her lap, pushing the spikes further into her underside. The screaming subsided as Elizabeth watched blood pouring off the chair in all directions. Within moments the girl was dead.

The two brutes smiled at each other. "At least we had fun with her before she died, eh, Jean?" Pierre said, his blackened teeth exposed.

Jean grabbed his crotch and said, "Best I've had in a long time."

They turned to Francois, who was lucky enough to be positioned away from seeing the girl's final moments. "Go ahead and confess, Huguenot," Jean, the deformed brute, said to Francois.

"I renounce my sins and will follow the true Catholic faith from now until eternity," Francois spat out as blood dripped from his mouth.

Jean and Pierre looked at each other and smiled grimly. "Confession at this point is pointless, Hugeonot. We've already found you guilty of your sins and are simply ridding your sickness from existence," Jean said. "There is no way out."

"No! No!" Francois yelled out as Pierre slowly turned the wooden crank of the rack, which pulled the ropes tighter on Francois's limbs.

"Papa!" Elizabeth yelled out as she watched from her cell.

Between his screams, Francois looked at his daughter, his eyes bulging from the pain. "Don't watch, Elizabeth! End it! Don't let them take…"

The crank went further, and there was a snap. Determined to witness her father's last moments, Elizabeth gathered herself in a way she never had before. She breathed deeply as her father's cries ceased and more cracks and snaps ensued. She watched as his arms were pulled out of his torso and his screaming stopped. Anger and hatred exploded within her at that moment. It was more than she ever knew was in her. The fetid air clung to her like a shroud, and the damp stone pressed against her back as she recoiled from the door, the chill seeping into her bones. The only solace was the glint of moonlight that speared through a high, barred window, etching a sliver of silver on the grimy floor.

The floor. She heard a clink and witnessed a sparkle near her father's remains. Neither of the brutes had noticed. Elizabeth strained her eyes to see what it was. A key had fallen out of his hand and reflected the moonlight in its silver brilliance. She had to reach it. It was the key to her home in Corveau. She wondered if she would ever see it again.

A sound, a ghoulish moan, sent a tremor through her. It seemed to emanate from the inky shadows, a chorus rising from the unseen depths of the dungeon.

Elizabeth strained to see, her heart hammering a frantic rhythm against her ribs.

Then, they materialized – wispy figures coalescing from the gloom. Men and women, their forms tattered and translucent, their faces etched with an eternal despair. They drifted around her, their ghostly limbs passing through the solid bars of her cell.

Elizabeth gasped, a strangled cry catching in her throat. One, a woman with hair the color of moonlight, drifted closer, her sorrowful eyes locking with Elizabeth's. Her lips moved, but no sound emerged, only a silent plea.

Panic clawed at Elizabeth's throat. Were these figments of her feverish imagination, hallucinations born of terror and despair? But no, the sorrow in their eyes, the cold touch of their ghostly forms against her skin – these were no mere phantoms. They were the ghosts of the condemned, she realized with a horrifying certainty. Souls trapped in this purgatory, testaments to the cruelty that resided within these very walls.

As if sensing her thoughts, the ghostly woman reached out a hand, its touch like a cold caress. Elizabeth flinched back, but the phantom hand passed through her, leaving a lingering sensation of immense power and unrivaled strength.

The chorus of moans intensified, a symphony of despair that echoed through the dank darkness. Elizabeth sank to the floor, burying her face in her knees, the sound a physical assault on her senses. She had just witnessed her father being torn apart.

Suddenly, a new presence appeared —a figure unlike the others shrouded in a darkness deeper than the dungeon itself. It pulsed with an unseen power, an evil energy sending chills skittering Elizabeth's spine. The other phantoms recoiled from it, their sorrowful moans turning to abject terror. The shadowy figure drifted towards her, its formless presence blocking the moonlight that had been her only solace.

Elizabeth squeezed her eyes shut, whispering a prayer she barely believed in any longer. She braced herself, convinced this was the end. But then, with a sound like a raven's shriek, the figure vanished. The haunting chorus resumed their mournful lament but with a newfound urgency as if urging her to flee.

Elizabeth, heart pounding, scrambled to her feet. Flee? But where could she go? She was trapped, a prisoner in this charnel house of the damned. As the cold tendrils of despair threatened to engulf her, a new resolve ignited within her. These spectral beings – they were proof of the cruelty that resided here. They were a testament to the darkness that she refused to succumb to. Drawing a ragged breath, she straightened her back. She may be trapped in this dungeon, but her spirit, she vowed, would not be broken. For the first time in her young life, she encountered the feeling of vengeance, and it excited her. Her sobbing ceased as a new energy pulsed through her veins. Was it God, or was it the cellar and the phantoms? Elizabeth did not care, for the vengeance consumed her like a barrel of wine. She smiled at the thought of exacting her revenge on her captors, the killers of the one love of her life - her dear father.

Two days had bled into one another, measured only by the gnawing in her belly and the relentless drip-drip of unseen water somewhere in the inky blackness. The bruisers, Pierre and Jean, had returned the night before, their laughter echoing through the stone like the howls of damned souls. They were drunk, their faces greasy with mutton fat and their breath reeking of sour wine.

"Still holding your tongue, little doll?" Pierre sneered, his voice raspy from ale. A single candle, sputtered to a nub, cast grotesque shadows that danced on the damp walls. Jean, the taller of the two, slammed a heavy steel saw down on the table, its teeth glinting predatorily.

Elizabeth, once a vibrant young woman with eyes the color of forget-me-nots, now resembled a wraith. Her once-fine gown was tattered, her unbound hair a tangled mess. Yet, beneath the grime and terror, a spark flickered in her gaze. The spark of a cornered beast had ignited into a terrifying resolve. "There is nothing left to confess," she rasped, her voice barely a whisper. "But you will die this day. I promise you."

She gave Jean a deviant grin as he advanced towards her. His hand shot out, thick fingers wrapping around her throat. The air was ripped from her lungs as he squeezed. Elizabeth's vision blurred, pinpricks of light dancing behind her closed eyelids.

Suddenly, a guttural growl arose from the shadows behind them. Pierre whirled around, his eyes widening in terror. A low moan echoed through the chamber, both primal and chilling. Elizabeth dared to open one eye. In the flickering candlelight, she saw it – a figure coalescing from the darkness. A giant figure.

Tall and skeletal, its form was shrouded in tattered robes. Its face, obscured by a hood, was a canvas of decay, the flesh stretched taut over a skull. A putrid stench, like a long-forgotten tomb, filled the air.

Jean let go of Elizabeth, recoiling as if struck. The creature took a lumbering step forward, its skeletal hand outstretched. Elizabeth saw a glint of metal in its bony grasp – a long, wickedly curved knife.

Panic battled with a strange sense of liberation in Elizabeth's chest. Had this apparition come to answer her silent prayers? Or was it a harbinger of a fate worse than death? Had she unknowingly made a pact with evil?

In a voice that sounded like stones grinding together, the creature spoke a single word—a word Elizabeth knew all too well, a word whispered in hushed tones amongst the villagers—"Revenant."

Pierre, his face slack with terror, fumbled for the saw. The creature's hand flickered. A flash of silver, a choked gurgle. In a heartbeat, Pierre lay sprawled on the floor, his jugular spurting a crimson fountain.

Jean, his eyes bulging from their sockets, backed away towards the barred door, his hand trembling on the iron latch. But it was too late. The creature, a whirlwind of skeletal fury, was upon him.

Elizabeth looked on with glee, willing to bear witness to the carnage.

The man's blood curdling scream ensued, followed by metal slicing through skin and bone. Gurgling blood from Jean's mouth ceased as a large volume of the dark liquid spilled onto the floor around the Revanant. The creature stood motionless, its task complete. Jean, like Pierre, lay lifeless, a grotesque parody of a man. However, his fate had been much worse. The Revanant stepped back and revealed Jean's body, cut in half lengthwise from his head to his crotch. The stench of death filled the air, mingling with the decaying essence of the Revenant.

Silence descended, broken only by the ragged gasps escaping Elizabeth's lips at seeing more unspeakable, yet satisfying, brutality. Was she free? Or had she simply traded one horror for another?

The answer came as the Revenant turned towards her. The hood fell back, revealing a skull devoid of flesh yet strangely familiar. Elizabeth gasped. Faint but unmistakable, the faded outline of a forget-me-not, her favorite flower, was etched upon the smooth forehead bone. At that moment, a horrifying truth dawned on her. The Revenant wasn't some monstrous spirit. The creature was her vengeance materialized and brought into existence, a vengeance for her father, wrought from the bonds of blood and a love that transcended the grave. What else could it be? Where did it come from? Did she manifest it?

A bony hand extended toward Elizabeth, and she recoiled. The wrist was exposed, stretched beyond the tattered black cloth barely covering the wraith. The Revenant's hand opened, and Elizabeth saw what it presented. In all its silver beauty, the skeleton key her father had held in death was a beacon of the home she may never see again. Elizabeth slowly reached out and took the key, her skin barely touching the bone of the creature's hand. With the metal firmly in her grasp, the Revenant faded into the darkness, its mission complete, its brief existence ended.

Elizabeth slumped against the damp wall, tears of terror and a chilling sense of triumph streaming down her face. She was free but at a terrible cost. The innocence she once possessed was as dead as Pierre and Jean. A cold resolve burned in its place, a pact made with the beyond. The world outside the dungeon walls might have seemed bleak before, but now, compared to the chilling covenant she had just likely forged, it held the allure of a forgotten paradise.

A moonless night, perfect for shadows, was her escape. With its creaking timbers and mournful sighs, Chateau de Mornay seemed to bid her farewell. The forest beyond, dark and forbidding, stretched out before her, a maw of unknown terrors. Yet, it was freedom, or at least a semblance of it.

Chapter Fifteen

The mountains, a jagged, unforgiving beast, were her destination. Legends spoke of it as a place of shadows and secrets, a home for the outcast and the damned. As she climbed, the wind whipped at her, a cruel caress that seemed to strip away the last vestiges of her former life.

Her refuge was a cave, a womb of stone, cold and indifferent. Here, in the heart of the mountain, she was alone. Or so she thought.

The nights were filled with echoes. Echoes of laughter, once joyous, now a haunting lament. Echoes of screams, her own and others, a cacophony of terror and madness. Visions danced before her eyes, fragments of a past she thought buried. There was the night of the torture and horrifying death of her father. Her hands, once soft and delicate, were gnarled and claw-like now. Once bright with youth, her eyes were now orbs of molten emeralds, filled with a terrifying and exhilarating sadness. She was changing, becoming something other than human.

The mountain was becoming her confessor, her accomplice. Its cold, hard embrace seemed to soothe the fires of her metamorphosis. In the depths of its heart, she found a strange peace, a twisted acceptance of her fate. She was no longer Elizabeth, the beautiful woman. She was becoming something else, something ancient and powerful—Eliza, the Mountain Witch.

As dawn approached, casting its pale light into the cave, she would sit by the mouth, watching the world below. Corveau, a streak of smoke on the horizon, was a constant reminder of her exile. But it was also a testament to her survival. She was an outcast, once a Protestant, but now a pariah, a witch. But she was alive. And in the heart of the mountain, she was free. Here, she was free to exact her revenge on the religious extremists who had destroyed her life. The mountain was her sanctuary, her prison, her mistress. Its heart, a hollow womb, held her secrets, her power, and her growing hunger. The woman she had once been was a fading memory, a ghost haunting the twilight of her consciousness. Now, she was something else, a creature of shadow, a witch born of despair and desolation.

She required certain elements, herbs, and stones to sustain her unnatural existence. The village of Corveau, once her home, now served as a necessary evil. Disguised poorly in the remnants of her former life, she would descend from the mountain, a specter amidst the living.

The Catholic villagers feared her, whispering of her as a creature of the night, a harbinger of ill omen. They were right, of course. But their fear was a shield, protecting them from the monstrous truth lurking in the shadows of their minds. The Catholics would normally arrest her immediately, but her visage was so terrible that they feared her and allowed her to roam the village as she needed, like a wild wolf strolling confidently through the streets, ready to kill in a heartbeat.

Her visits were brief and calculated. She moved through the marketplace like a shadow, her eyes cold and distant. The touch of a conjured coin was anathema to her, but she willingly paid the price for the ingredients that fueled her dark arts.

Returning to the mountain was a relief. The ascent was a pilgrimage, a return to the sacred. With its perpetual twilight, the cave welcomed her with a silent embrace. She felt at home, surrounded by the relics of her transformation. But the mountain offered more than a sanctuary. It provided sustenance. The occasional wanderer, lured by false promises of a shortcut, would stumble upon her domain. These were her feasts, dark and unholy sacraments. Sometimes adults, but often children. All of them were enemies. All of them were responsible for her downfall.

With a feral grace born of necessity, she would strike. Once the temple of the soul, the flesh became a mere vessel to be consumed. The stripped bones were added to her growing collection, a macabre altar to her transformation. A fire and spit cooked her fresh human meat.

In the quiet moments between these savage acts, she would turn to her spells, her incantations. She spoke to the wind, commanded the earth, and bargained with shadows. Her voice, once melodious, was now a rasping croak, a language born of the abyss.

With each passing moon, her power grew, her form more grotesque. The woman was fading, replaced by a creature of myth and nightmare. Yet, a flicker of humanity remained in the depths of her monstrous existence. A longing for companionship, love, and a desire to escape eternal solitude. Her father's love and tinges of happiness struck her dwindling humanity. But these were delusions, fleeting moments of weakness in a world of shadow and bone. The mountain was her home now, and the darkness was her only companion.

The mountain was more than a refuge; it was a library of secrets. Within its heart, in the labyrinthine depths of her cavernous dwelling, Eliza had discovered a nexus of power. Here, the veil between the living and the dead was thin, and the echoes of ancient magic hung heavy in the air.

It was in these moments of profound solitude that she began to hear them. At first, faint whispers, like the rustle of dry leaves in an autumn wind. Then, clear and distinct voices carried on the currents of the mountain's breath. They were the voices of her sisters, the witches of old, a coven bound by blood and sorcery across millennia.

Among them was a voice that resonated with a particular authority as ancient as the mountains. It was the voice of Pythia, the Pythoness, the original human sorceress from Ancient Greek mythology. She was the oracle of Delphi, her giant serpent slayed by Apollo on his quest for greatness as he claimed Delphi for his own. Pythia's words were a balm to Elizabeth's tormented soul, a map through the labyrinth of her transformation.

"You are not alone, child of shadows," Pythia's voice echoed in the cavern. "We watch over you, as you will watch over those who come after. Your dark path is fraught with peril, but within you lies a power beyond measure. No creature can stand before you in their wrath. I will be your guide. Call, child, when you desire my counsel."

With each passing day, Eliza delved deeper into this ethereal communion. She learned more about herbs and stones, celestial alignments, and lunar cycles. She was taught the ancient tongue, a language as old as time, in which the universe's secrets were encoded. The echoes of her chanting emitted from the cave, and all living creatures fled the area. The cave became a crucible, a place of both torment and enlightenment. As her physical form withered, her spirit expanded. She could feel the world around her, a tangled web of energy pulsing with life. She saw the future, a kaleidoscope of glorious and terrifying possibilities. She also saw the past and present together. Time was no longer linear. Eliza was freshly born, knowing her entire existence, and every moment was no surprise.

But with this newfound power came a heavy burden. It seemed that the weight of the world rested upon her shoulders. She was a guardian, a protector, and a destroyer. The balance of nature, the delicate interplay of light and dark, depended on her. She was a new Oracle, and the mountain was her Delphi, or so she desired.

The isolation, once a solace, now felt like a prison. The mountain, once a loving mother, now seemed a demanding taskmaster. Yet, she persevered, driven by a purpose that transcended her existence.

In the quiet hours of the night, Eliza would sit in meditation, her mind a vast expanse where the spirits of her ancestors gathered. They were a council of wisdom, a sorority of shadows. And, at the center of it all was Pythia, the eternal guide, the first and greatest.

The Greek pythoness spoke in an enchanting, intoxicating voice as her spectral form appeared in billowing white robes. At first, she was a blurred abstraction of humanity, but then her beauty came, leaving Eliza with a sick feeling. Pythia's beauty contrasted her decay. Eliza's face was gray, with black veins breaking through the light skin like a river through a ravine. Her hair was raven black and shiny, probably the only beauty left on her, save for two enchanting green eyes.

Pythia spoke. "A true dark witch does not abide by time. It means nothing to her. She has even witnessed her death yet has no control over its occurrence. No matter what she tries to alter, her death will remain the same. It is like she drops a pebble in the water, hoping to adjust its serene nature. She is dropping that pebble in another lake at a different time. She is bound by fate, a true prisoner thereof. That witch doesn't think for herself but is a conduit of The Dark. The

Dark Witch does its bidding and can go anywhere at any time. Heed my words, sister."

Then Eliza spoke in her crackling, strained voice. "The Dark Witch needs no grimoire. She has memorized it all over the centuries. All the incantations and spells are already in her. She needs no book. She is the book." The words were in her, and she spoke them without realizing what she had said. But the words gave her pride and strength, and Pythia smiled brightly at Eliza like a proud mother.

Eliza was becoming more than a witch. She was becoming a nexus, a living conduit for ancient magic. The transformation was painful, but in the heart of it, there was a strange exhilaration. She was evolving, ascending, becoming something beyond human comprehension. The energy that coursed through her was boundless, intoxicating, and addictive. And all of it was born from the torturous, deadly cellar of Chateau de Mornay.

Chapter Sixteen

The wind howled like a wounded beast, its mournful dirge a chilling accompaniment to Eliza's journey. The mountain peaks, once familiar and comforting, now loomed as menacing giants, their icy breath promising oblivion. Yet, the allure of the abyss pulled her onward. She was no longer the trembling girl they had made but a creature of shadow and storm, a witch of the darkest mountains.

The Chateau de Mornay, once a gilded cage of torment, now stood as a skeletal monument to her past. Its turrets, once spires of mockery, were now shrouded in a perpetual twilight. The air was thick with the scent of decay and desperation, a haze that clung to her like a suffocating embrace.

Weeks went by in the mountains. Then, with a strength born of despair, Eliza ascended the steps of the chateau. Each stone was a wraith of pain, each shadow a specter of her former self. Inside, the grand halls were now caverns of echoing silence. The air was cold and still. The only sound was the insistent drip of unseen water. Eliza saw the chateau as Anna and Brad had seen it the first day. However, the chateau should be golden and unmatched. Why this dark dwelling?

The residents of the chateau, the de Mornays, the two demented torturers, were now dead. The chateau was hers. Eliza entered her new home and felt her power surge like never before. She wandered the desolate chateau like a phantasm, absorbing every detail. The beautiful furniture, the gilded walls—everything was gone. Then a faint sound upstairs gave her pause. A voice and footsteps. But who? Eliza ascended the grand staircase in the foyer and rushed toward the source of her broken, beloved silence. There, inside the great bedroom she saw the fresco of Lazarus, and a man, frozen in his steps upon spotting the tattered witch before him.

Eliza spoke first, her voice low and authoritative. "Who are you?"

"I am Dubois de Mornay. You are a trespasser in my home." Although not quite as hideous as the other two de Mornays that the Revenant had murdered, Dubois had an unfavorable look to him and reminded Eliza of his kin and what they had done to her father.

"On the contrary, you are trespassing in *my* home," Eliza hissed as she approached Dubois.

He saw the grotesque features of her wrinkled face and backed away toward the enormous bed.

Eliza continued toward him and Dubois unsheathed a sword for defense. She cackled as she spun an enchantment in the air like floating molten gold. It was circular with strange rune patterns inside. Suddenly the sword launched from Dubois' hand and flew through the enormous room, gaining speed. Surprised by the witch's work, he never saw the sword fly blindingly fast toward him. With a thud, the sword impaled his chest, the hilt of the weapon stopping at his breastbone. He looked down at the blood growing on his shirt and back at Eliza, who smiled at her handiwork. Unexpectedly, the sword reversed and flew through the air again, depositing crimson droplets throughout the room as it gained speed. Still in shock, Dubois watched as the sword launched into his abdomen, the steel blade protruding from his back. He began to stumble as Eliza grinned before him, her arms hidden in her cloak and the golden runes still floating before her.

"What is this demon magic?" Dubois spluttered as he stumbled, trying to stay upright with pride.

"It is practice," Eliza crowed as the sword recoiled and repeated its deadly dance around the room. Suddenly, the sword flew into Dubois's mouth, slowed, and turned downward as it traveled down his throat until the hilt clinked against his teeth, shattering them with its force. The doomed man reached toward Eliza in desperation before dropping lifeless to the floor next to the bed. A large pool of blood spread beneath him, staining the floor in that spot for hundreds of years, for Anna and Brad to notice on their tour.

In the heart of the chateau cellar, a chamber awaited Eliza. It was here, in this very room, that they had stripped her of her spirit, her hope, her very name. Now, it would be the altar of her rebirth. The moon, an evil eye, cast its eerie glow upon the chamber, illuminating the ancient symbols etched into the floor. These were not man's work but of a power older than time, which she now sought to harness.

With a trembling hand, she touched the cold stone. A surge of darkness coursed through her veins, a familiar yet exhilarating agony. Images flashed before her eyes - the rack, the cruel laughter of her tormentors, her father's skeleton key, the chateau on fire, crowds invading the home, a beautiful blonde woman bathing in the bedroom. But these were not to consume her. Instead, they fueled her into a potent elixir of rage and determination.

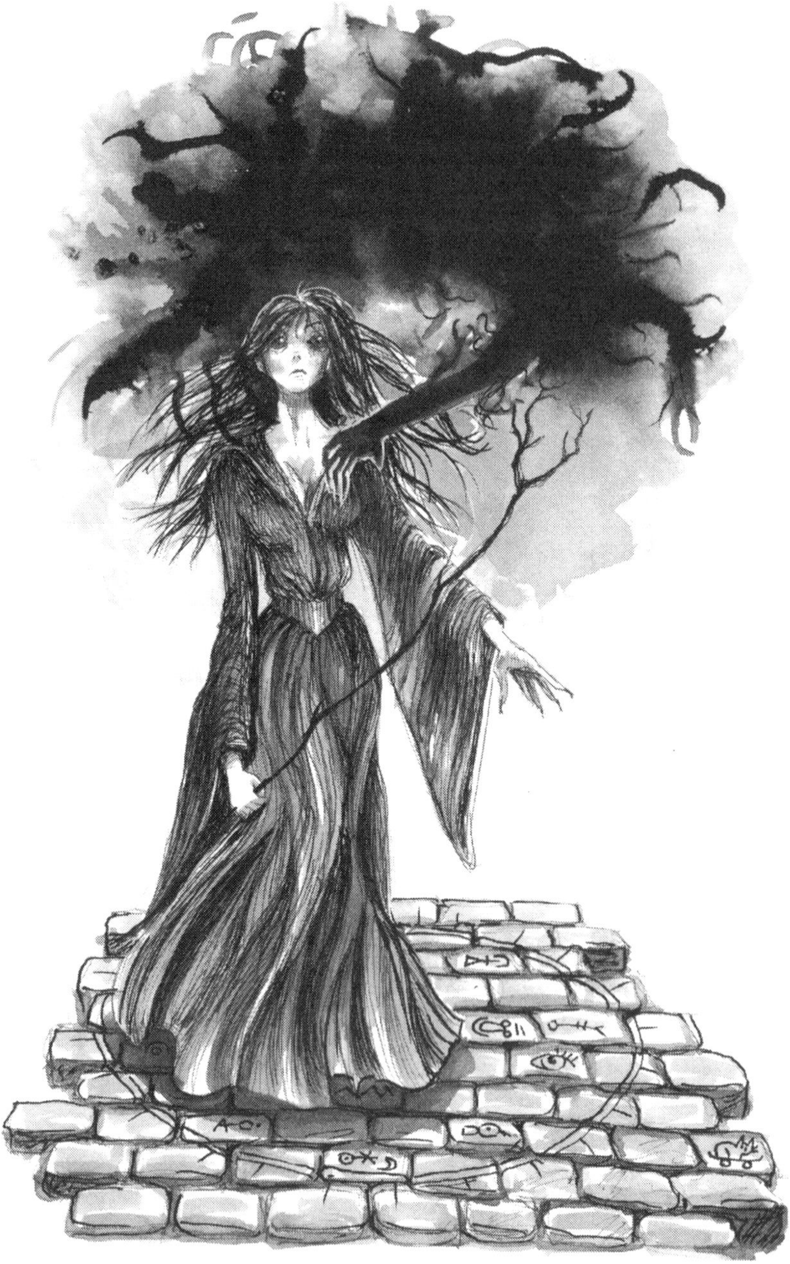

As the night deepened, so did Eliza's communion with the darkness. The wind outside grew into a storm, and the chateau creaked and groaned in response. In the heart of this maelstrom, she stood, a solitary figure against the onslaught of the elements. Yet, she was not afraid. For in this chaos, she found order. In this desolation, she found power.

And then, a voice, deep and resonant, echoed through the chamber. It was a voice of promise, of terrible beauty, a voice that spoke of dominion and destruction. It was the voice of The Dark, calling to her, claiming her as its own. The soundwaves had no source. The Dark spoke to her from everywhere. Even as she exited the cellar and inspected her new home, The Dark stood by her. She always felt it, like a reassuring hand on her shoulder, reminding her that it held dominion, not her. Eliza rarely spoke, but she was often curious about the source of The Dark as she wandered alone through the chateau. "Where did you come from? Were you here before me?"

"*Oui. Oui. Je suis plus âgé que le château. Je suis venu ici pour me nourrir et grandir. Vous m'avez donné une nouvelle vie.*" Yes. Yes. I am older than the chateau. I came here to feed and grow. You have given me a new life.

"How has this been accomplished?" Eliza asked, her voice always gravely and low.

The deep, sourceless voice boomed, "Your pain was greater than those before you. Many died here. The suffering and death sustained me until you, Eliza. You were born with a power within you. It merely needed to be pushed further."

"What do you need from me?" she asked.

"Sustain me. Give me everything you can. Feed me fear, suffering, and evil. I will grow. We will grow together."

Eliza smiled. "Together," she replied.

The following night, Eliza, the dark sorceress, stood at the precipice of a new era. Her power, she wanted more. The Dark needed more. She knew it required a sacrifice to ascend further and become truly invincible. A pure sacrifice, a vessel untouched by the shame of darkness.

Her choice fell upon a young girl, a creature of light and innocence. Her name was Anya, and she was the daughter of a local peasant family. Eliza had observed her from afar in her travels into town, a radiant beacon in the sea of human depravity.

With a cunning plan, she lured Anya to the Chateau de Mornay, promising the girl a life of luxury and adventure. The chateau, once a symbol of power, now served as a trap, a gilded cage.

Anya, with her heart full of hope and her eyes sparkling with wonder, followed Eliza into the silent halls. The chateau, with its creaking floors and echoing chambers, seemed to whisper of secrets and danger. But Anya pressed on, oblivious to the darkness within its walls.

Eliza led the girl to the heart of the chateau, the ballroom filled with strange symbols and arcane artifacts. At the center of the room stood a cauldron bubbling with a sinister green brew. "This is a place of great power," Eliza said, her voice dripping with false charm. "And you, Anya, are destined to be a part of it."

Anya's eyes widened with excitement. "What must I do?" she asked, her voice trembling with anticipation.

Eliza smiled a cruel, predatory grin. But her voice was changed into something sweet, tinged with honey for the young girl. "You must sacrifice yourself, Anya. Give your life to The Dark; in return, you will be reborn, more powerful than ever."

With a sweet heart lured by lies, Anya stepped towards the cauldron. As she reached out to touch the bubbling brew, Eliza struck. A sharp and cold dagger pierced Anya's heart. The girl's eyes widened in disbelief, her face contorting in pain. Eliza's face glowed green from the bubbling cauldron, her grin an explosion of greed and power.

Anya fell to the ground, her lifeblood staining the ballroom floor. Eliza stood over her, her eyes filled with a strange, almost disappointed, expression. She had expected a surge of power, a rush of dark energy. But nothing came. The sacrifice had failed.

Eliza knelt beside Anya's lifeless body, her fingers tracing the cold contours of the dagger. She had underestimated the power of innocence and the human spirit's purity. No matter how vast, the darkness within her could not consume such a light.

A wave of despair washed over Eliza. She had lost her chance to ascend to a higher plane of existence. She was trapped, a prisoner of her darkness.

With a heavy heart, she turned away from Anya's body. Once a place of power, the chateau now felt like a tomb. The darkness that had once fueled her was now a suffocating weight.

As she left the room, she glanced back at Anya. The girl's face, serene in death, seemed to blame her. Eliza felt a pang of guilt, a fleeting moment of remorse. But it was quickly overshadowed by a cold, calculating resolve. She turned back and hefted the innocent girl's body into the glowing green cauldron, splashing the deadly concoction on the ballroom floor. Within moments, Anya's body had dissolved into the bitter mix.

The sacrifice had failed, but her quest was not over. She would find another way, a darker path. And if she couldn't ascend through purity, she would do so through depravity. The darkness within her was vast, and it was only beginning to awaken.

Hush, my dear, the moon is high,
Stars like daggers in the sky.
But shadows dance and whispers creep,
While wicked witches softly sleep.
With eyes of jade and hair like night,
She stirs her cauldron, pale moonlight.
Frogs and toads, a slimy crew,
Stir the brew, both old and new.
She chants a spell, a chilling sound,
As cobwebs weave and ghosts abound.
Beware the woods, where shadows play,
The witch is near, she'll steal your day.
So close your eyes and sleep so tight,
Let nightmares flee in moonless night.
For if she finds you, small and frail,
She'll cast a spell, and you will wail.

Chapter Seventeen

The night was as black as the depths of the soul, save for the faint glow of a waning moon that cast eerie shadows upon the cobbled streets of Corveau. Eliza moved through the village silently, her emerald eyes glinting in the gloom. Her long, black hair, streaked with wisps of gray, flowed behind her like a raven's wing.

Her target was Father Sebastien, a man of God known for his unwavering faith and kindness. Eliza had heard tales of his compassion, his ability to soothe troubled souls. This very strength made him the perfect vessel for her dark ambitions. He was also a Catholic, and his kind had mutilated her father and sent her on this journey of vengeance and despair.

She found the priest in his small, candlelit cottage. She lulled him into a deep slumber with a whisper of a spell, then carried him away, his body as light as a feather in her powerful grasp. She carried him through the mist-covered streets, seen by a few citizens who cowered away upon glancing at her glowing green eyes like she was Medusa reborn. They dared not speak of what they saw.

The Chateau de Mornay, a now-abandoned home to nothing except death and torture on the outskirts of the village, was Eliza's new lair. The priest stirred as she descended the winding staircase into the damp, musty cellar.

His eyes, filled with fear, met hers. "Woman," he gasped, his voice trembling. "What do you want?"

The witch smiled, a chilling, inhuman display of joy. "I want your soul, Father Sebastien," she replied, her voice a low, seductive purr.

The priest's face paled. "You cannot take my soul," he cried, his voice rising in desperation. "I am a servant of God!"

Eliza's smile widened. "Oh, but I can," she said, her eyes glowing with a sinister light. "Call to your Lord. Bring him forth so that I can consume his soul as well."

The terror in the priest's voice doubled as he said, "you're the Mountain Witch! God help me!"

"Yes. Call to him," Eliza said. With a flick of her wrist, she summoned the series of grotesque metal contraptions that she had seen used before in her former life. They were devices of torture designed to inflict extreme pain and suffering. The priest's eyes widened in horror as she adjusted the machines.

"No!" he screamed, his voice filled with terror. "Please, have mercy!"

But Eliza was deaf to his pleas. With a cruel twist of her hand, she activated the machines. The priest's screams echoed through the cellar, a chilling symphony of pain and despair. His body contorted and writhed, his spirit slowly being crushed beneath the weight of his torment. His body floated between each machine, lifted aloft by Eliza's spell. First was the rack, where the ropes tied themselves, and the gear had no master. The machine did its awful work, and the priest screamed in tremendous pain. Then it was the chair, spikes slicing into his thighs through his frock, formerly brown and now covered in blood. As he grew weaker, his body went limp. Finally, Eliza floated him into the Iron Maiden, a metal upright casket filled with spikes.

Eliza waved her hand, and the door slammed shut, the last screams muffled inside the casket. Once the door closed, it was instant death from spikes entering his eyes, nose, and mouth.

As the priest's final breath escaped him, a power surge coursed through Eliza. A streaming cloud of white exited the priest's mouth through the maiden of death, and entered her.

She felt her dark magic growing, expanding, reaching new and terrifying heights. She had absorbed the life force of a man of faith, a vessel of divine power. And now, she was more powerful than she had ever dreamed.

Thoughts of her being held captive and her father's torture in that very chamber were mere remnants in her mind, memories fading quickly from the evil within her. The vengeance born inside her from that horrendous day, wreaked havoc on any goodness in her. Nothing remained except The Dark.

The Chateau de Mornay became her fortress, a place of darkness, despair, and solitude. And from its shadows, she would spread her influence, casting a pall of terror over the land. The reign of the Mountain Witch had begun three hundred years before the spirit of Luc de Mornay killed Vivienne Laurent for her lion's heart.

Chapter Eighteen

Eliza brazenly continued her saunterings into Corveau, but only at night. She learned that the daytime lowered her power and angered her. The moon was her new sun. The brighter it became, the more it fueled her horrendous strength. She liked to taunt the citizens at night, giggling madly as she made her way through the shadows. She became a legend, something that parents told their children about. "If you are bad, the Mountain Witch will find you," they said, and they meant it. They had all seen her. The fear she coaxed pleased and fulfilled Eliza. Nobody dared get her attention or speak to her as she haunted the streets.

But then a man called out to her on one of her excursions into the night. He was drunk, but not a drunkard. The man was dressed well, and she was shocked that he had called out to her.

Eliza saw that he was alone from across the stone street. In a second, she was inches from him. The man gasped and smiled after he saw the detail of Eliza's face. She had changed her previous ghastly form into an unavoidable young teenage beauty with the softest skin and most favored lips.

The man tried to speak, but Eliza touched his mouth. "Fuck me," she whispered in his ear, her voice sweet and lustful.

The man gasped, followed quickly by a grin of pleasure. The word was rarely spoken, but he knew what she meant.

Eliza took his hand, and they fled into the shadows. Although now a creature of darkness, she was still a virgin, and she yearned for sensual pleasure. She lusted after both men and women, sometimes touching herself in the shadows of the streets underneath her cloak. She would moan and laugh, and the citizens fled with their blood as frozen as the peaks of the nearby Pyrenees Mountains.

On this night, however, she stroked the man's hardness, and it made her ravenous as they lay in a storage building filled with farming tools. There was no light, save for Eliza's eyes glowing green.

The alcohol flowing through the man made him not care about the strange behavior of this woman. He didn't know who she was. All he knew was that she was beautiful and wanting to lay with him. That was all he needed.

Within moments, Eliza straddled him. She screamed out in pain and ecstasy as her hymen broke and she bled.

The man felt it but cared not. All he wanted to do was finish and tell his friends about taking a young virgin in the tool shack.

Eliza rode him as they both moaned. The man reached into her cloak and squeezed her bare breasts, ice cold to the touch. Unnaturally cold. Within moments, they orgasmed together, and Eliza felt the hot semen shoot inside her, mixing with her blood.

"Do you like young girls?" she asked as she looked down at his face, barely lit by the moonlight.

"Yes, of course I do. Will you marry me?" he asked half-drunkenly but also fully serious.

Eliza laughed uproariously as the man fondled her breasts. Within moments, she began to change. His hands weren't touching the breasts of a young woman anymore, but rather an old hag, her breasts sagging and used. Eliza's form had reverted, and her laugh became sick and twisted. "Marry you? No, my beautiful man. I am going to kill you," she sneered.

The man's eyes widened as terror coursed through his body. Just as he was about to push her off him, a scythe flew through the shed with lightning speed. He gasped as the scythe passed by.

Later that night, Eliza continued her haunting of Corveau, but now with a renewed sense of pleasure. The hag giggled like a young girl and twirled in the street. Onlookers stayed in the shadows to avoid contact or even a gaze from the Mountain Witch.

Her mirthful twirls continued as her arms stretched out. Hanging from her hand was the man's head by his hair, perfectly severed by the scythe before he even knew it. She let go of the head mid-twirl, and it rolled down the street with a grotesque squishy sound as it hit the stone road.

The citizens who witnessed it gasped and ran off.

"Bring me more, Corveau! Bring all your God-fearing, trembling cowards to me! I will set them free!" Eliza yelled out to the empty street.

Near dawn, the wind howled through the shattered windows of Chateau de Mornay, a mournful dirge that echoed through the empty halls. Eliza wandered through the vast, decaying edifice, her footsteps muffled by the thick layers of dust and debris. Her emerald eyes, glowing in the dim light, scanned the crumbling walls, their peeling paint, wallpaper, and exposed wood, starkly similar to the ripped black cloak that draped her form. She realized she was witnessing the chateau's changes through time. Objects went through entire life cycles before her eyes. She knew the life and destruction of everything near her. A vile grin crossed her face as she realized it was a new power brought to her by the priest's death.

A chill ran through the witch as she entered the grand ballroom. The room had once been opulent, its walls adorned with faded tapestries and its ceiling supported by an ornate chandelier. Now, it was a cavern of darkness, filled with the whispers of ancient dancing spirits and the echo of her footsteps. The enormous chandelier vibrated from her power as she walked under it. She was inside the chateau's future, perhaps hundreds of years away. Why? She did not yet know.

Near a glowing green cauldron, that aided her spells, a shadowy figure stood in the center of the ballroom, twelve feet tall and cloaked in even deeper darkness than Eliza's own. It was The Dark, her mistress, the entity that had rescued and granted her power. She had never seen it in its present form, and it even gave her pause in its dark void within the cloak. Could it be the Revenant that helped her before?

"The Revenant was my form from very long ago. You are beginning to see through time. Even I have a beginning and end. Do you see it?" The Dark's feminine voice boomed and echoed in the ballroom.

Eliza closed her eyes. "Yes, mistress. I see your end," she said.

A deep and horrible laugh emanated from the creature. "And I have seen your end," it said. "You have done well," The Dark's voice rumbled, a deep, guttural sound that seemed to emanate from the chateau's very depths.

Eliza knelt before the giant creature, her head bowed. "It is my duty, mistress," she replied, her voice barely a whisper.

"The villagers of Corveau retain faith," The Dark continued. "Their faith is a thorn in my side. It is time to remind them of the true power in the shadows. Give them their fate."

Eliza's heart pounded with excitement. "As you command, mistress," she said.

"Bring me more souls," The Dark ordered. "Sacrifice them to me, and your power shall grow."

Eliza rose to her feet, her eyes filled with a chilling determination. She would not fail her mistress. She would bring her the souls she desired, no matter the cost.

As she turned to leave the chamber, a sudden gust of wind blew through the room, lifting the curtains and revealing a sliver of dawning sunlight that illuminated a small, dusty mirror hanging on the wall. Eliza caught her reflection, and a shiver ran down her spine. Her eyes, usually so blue and vibrant, were green and lifeless in the pale light. Her beauty had faded. She had felt it, but this was a rare reminder of her new form. She shuddered, knowing the young woman she once was no longer existed. Her once delicate white skin now looked rotten and gray, with black veins visible everywhere. She touched her cold face. A single tear rolled down her cheek, but she quickly wiped it away, her resolve hardening. She had a duty to fulfil, a mistress to serve. The villagers of Corveau would pay the price for their faith in God.

Chapter Nineteen

The sky above Corveau had been ominous and inky black for days. The superstitious villagers whispered about impending doom, fearing the wrath of God would descend upon their peaceful hamlet for unknown sins. Unbeknownst to them, their fears were rooted in a much more sinister reality. Eliza, the Mountain Witch, was coming.

As the first tendrils of a storm began to lash at the village, the villagers huddled together, their prayers rising to a silent sky. But their pleas were met with a deafening roar as lightning crackled across the heavens, illuminating the terrified faces of the townspeople.

Eliza stood at the edge of the village, her silhouette outlined against the storm-tossed sky. She raised her arms, and a storm erupted around her, winds whipping through the streets, tearing down houses and uprooting trees. Rain fell in torrents, turning the cobbled streets into rivers and sweeping away everything in its path.

The villagers, terrified and helpless, fled for their lives, their cries lost in the howling wind. But Eliza was relentless. She sent lightning bolts crashing down from the sky, striking buildings and people alike. The village was transformed into a scene of utter devastation, a testament to her power and malice.

Soldiers, their muskets raised, fired at her, balls piercing her body. But she merely laughed, the pain a distant sensation as she continued to wreak havoc. The balls passed through her, leaving no trace, a testament to the dark magic that protected her.

The Dark, her mistress, spoke to her from the growing clouds, filling her with a sense of infinite power. "Let them know the true meaning of your wrath."

And Eliza obeyed. She felt the strength blast through her body, remembering her father and the cruelty she had witnessed in her former life. Her power grew to an apex. She unleashed a final, devastating spell, a storm of darkness that engulfed the village. Her voice boomed through the region, uttering words in ancient languages. It was a tornado but completely black; anything entering it disappeared completely in the swirling gyre. The villagers, trapped in the storm's heart, were consumed by the darkness, their screams lost to the wind.

When the storm finally passed, Corveau was a desolate wasteland, a stark reminder of Eliza's vengeance. The villagers, once a proud and devout community, were no more. And Eliza, the dark witch, stood triumphant, her heart filled with a cold, empty satisfaction. They were her enemy. Their cruelty had forced her people out of Corveau and many to execution. The villagers deserved to be shredded by the storm.

Most buildings stood, but the storm had taken every living soul. Legend would linger that the villagers were taken by God's wrath rather than a single woman's vengeance.

Chapter Twenty

After razing the village, Eliza returned to Chateau de Mornay, her new home, where she now ruled the region. She paused at the cellar entrance, her heart thrumming against her ribcage as she hesitated to step into the depths of the familiar abode. The air, laden with the scent of damp earth and decay, sent a shiver down her spine, invoking memories that clawed at the edges of her mind.

With a deep breath, she crossed the threshold, the heavy door creaking like a lamentation from the past. She descended into the cellar, the stairs steep and treacherous, each footfall echoing ominously in the dark. As she reached the bottom, the chill enveloped her like a shroud, and the faint light of a single, flickering torch cast jagged silhouettes upon the rough stone walls.

It was here that she had seen her father ripped apart, where so many had suffered before death. In this dim recess, she now beheld her mistress, The Dark, the entity that had guided her hand.

Emerging from the shadows, The Dark loomed before her, more visible now than ever—a hulking figure twice as tall as a man, draped in tattered black fabric, the folds of its cloak swaying like the whispers of lost souls. A hood concealed its features, but two piercing red eyes glowed like embers in the depths of a forgotten grave. The loose, shredded fabric blew in an unseen wind. The sight was enough to chill Eliza's blood, and she felt rooted to the spot as if the earth had conspired to hold her in thrall.

"What brings you back, Eliza?" The Dark's voice reverberated through the cellar, low and booming, echoing with the weight of centuries. It spoke like the shadows had conspired to form words, and Eliza's heart raced as she found her voice.

"I— I was compelled to return," she stammered, eyes wide with fear. Even she was terrified of the creature before her. "I wished to know if—"

"Your work in the old world is finished." The Dark's words fell like a verdict, echoing with finality. The haunting figure took a step forward, and Eliza recoiled instinctively. The cloak parted just slightly, revealing a black corset and gown of medieval design, cinched tightly against decayed flesh, gray and rotting, as if the very essence of life had long since fled. The corset pushed up her mistress's cleavage into a gray heap that would have been attractive if not belonging to the hideous being.

"What do you mean?" Eliza's voice quivered, her mind racing. "I thought—"

"'You thought to linger in a world that no longer beckons you?" The Dark interrupted, its presence oppressive and suffocating. "You destroyed the entire village for me, and I am thankful and more powerful. I came from this land during the harrowing plague when the Black Death swept through France like a ravenous beast, claiming souls for its dark banquet. I was born of that despair, woven from the shadows that danced in the light of countless extinguished lives.'

'I recall the sweet fragrance of life before the shadows enveloped my world—a time when laughter danced through the air like sunlight upon the dewy grass. My name was Celine, a name that once sang of heaven's promise, whispering of purity and grace. But the fates conspired cruelly, twisting into something monstrous, and I became a harbinger of despair amidst the relentless tide of the Black Death.'

'The year was 1348, and the air was heavy with the stench of decay, punctuated by the wails of the afflicted. As the illness gripped my village, I felt my body surrender to its insidious touch, a fever blazing within me like a devil's fire. I was merely a girl of seventeen, my heart still naive and yearning for the warmth of love, yet the specter of death loomed ever closer, its skeletal hand reaching out to claim me.'

'In those harrowing days, as my skin turned clammy and my breath came in ragged gasps, I bore witness to the chaos surrounding me. The streets were lined with the dead—my friends, my family—discarded like so much refuse, their cries silenced beneath the weight of the plague's relentless grip. In my delirium, I begged for mercy, but it was denied. My body rotted from within, my once radiant form withering under the plague's dreadful reign.'

'When I finally succumbed, my lifeless body was tossed onto a cart with others, a macabre procession of the forsaken. I drifted into a dreamless void, feeling neither pain nor the fleeting memories of joy. But within that abyss of despair, something stirred. The suffering around me resonated, weaving through the air like magic, drawing forth a power I could not comprehend. I felt the pulse of anguish reverberate, and at that moment, I was reborn—not as the heavenly Celine, but as a monstrous entity wrought from the very fabric of despair.'

'I awoke within the depths of night, cloaked in shadow, my once-human form transformed into a towering phantom, draped in a tattered shroud that billowed like smoke. My eyes, now glowing embers of crimson fire, pierced the darkness with an insatiable hunger. I was not merely alive; I was an embodiment of death itself, a vengeful spirit awakened from the grave.'

'In those shadowy hours, I felt the pulse of the plague as it ravaged the land, and I reveled in the chaos it brought. I wandered the lonely streets of France, where the living fled in terror from death. They saw me as a remnant of their fears, a vision that confirmed their darkest imaginings. As the grim reaper of their nightmares, I found a wicked delight in the power I wielded. They cried to God, and I laughed at them.'

'Oh, how the village quaked at the sight of me! I wove through the shadows, committing my gruesome deeds hidden beneath the cloak of the plague. Under the cover of night, I would hunt those whose lives were untouched, extinguishing their flickering flames one by one. They would vanish into the darkness, their screams swallowed by the night, their existence erased as if they had never been. I became much stronger with each kill, an artisan of death, fashioning my craft from the very horrors I had once endured.'

'The villagers whispered tales of a dark spirit—a creature that haunted the dying, preying upon their fears. I had embraced the chaos, feasting on the thick despair in the air. Each life I claimed only strengthened me, fueling my shadowy ascent as I danced upon the graves of the fallen. I became a cyclone, an embodiment of the plague's cruel hand. The very earth trembled beneath my feet, and I rejoiced in the anguish I spread. Where I tread, death followed; where I roamed, hope withered. I was no longer a girl yearning for love; I had become the darkness incarnate, a figure whose essence thrived on the pain of the living—and dying.'

'As I look back upon my unholy transformation, I marvel at the bitter irony of my existence. Celine, the heavenly child, had been reborn as a creature of torment. The angels above wept for me, but their tears fell upon deaf ears, for I had severed all ties to the light.'

'In this twilight realm, I stand eternal, a testament to the shadows within every heart. The Black Death is but a memory now, yet I remain—a lingering specter of suffering, a phantom born of despair, forever haunting the ruins of my former life. And as the darkness stretches out before me, I smile, for I know that I shall reign undying, a cruel reminder that even the most celestial can fall into the abyss.'"

Eliza felt her breath quicken, overwhelmed by the history that clung to The Dark like an ancient shroud. "But... but I have much left to do here! There are secrets yet to unveil, mysteries waiting in the quiet corners of this world."

The Dark inclined its head, the hood shifting slightly, allowing a glimpse of the grinning skull beneath—a macabre visage that sent another tremor through her. "What you seek is but an echo of the past. The true path lies beyond the seas, in a land where your fate awaits. You must book passage to the New World, where you shall remain until the call draws you back to this place."

"Across the sea?" Eliza echoed, disbelief mingling with dread. "Why must I leave? What purpose lies in such a journey?"

"Do you not see?" The Dark leaned closer, her voice a thunderous whisper reverberating through the stones. "You are part of a design far greater than your understanding. The blood that courses through your veins is intertwined with the fates of those who have come before you—and will come after. Your presence here has stirred the echoes, awakened the slumbering shadows, and now you must follow where the tide beckons. The pious have fled to the New World, unguarded and faithful. They are ripe for your reaping, Eliza."

The air thickened, pressing against Eliza's chest as if the weight of inevitability bore down upon her. A part of her longed to resist, to scream against the darkness that sought to dictate her future, yet another part—the part that had yearned for knowledge and power—was drawn to the promise of what lay beyond the horizon. "Will I be alone?" she whispered, her voice barely a breath in the cavernous space.

The Dark straightened, towering over her, the threads of its cloak stretching like tendrils of night. "You are never truly alone, Eliza. The shadows will follow, and you will find companions in the darkness in time, for many are waiting for you. Book your passage, for the winds of fate are already shifting."

With that, the Dark receded into the shadows, leaving Eliza trembling in the cold grip of the cellar, grappling with a sense of purpose and foreboding that weighed heavily upon her spirit. She turned toward the stairs, her mind whirling with the knowledge of her fate, as she ascended back into the light of the moon, carrying with her the burden of an uncertain destiny.

Chapter Twenty One

In death, Anna found herself standing at the gate of a beautiful mansion, its architectural facade a reminder that she was in modern times. The night was a living thing, cloaked in the heavy embrace of fog that rolled off the sea, curling like ghostly fingers around the new houses of the peninsula town of Castine, Maine. A moment ago, she had been with Etienne, a sword hilt protruding from her chest. Now she was in a familiar location wearing a black formal gown that flowed in the ocean breeze. Why did she know this place? Anna knew she had never been to this area before.

As the wind howled, she felt a familiar dread settle in her bones, for she was entangled within a web of dark magic. She was bound by the will of the one whose shadow loomed over centuries like a specter refusing to fade. Anna sensed that her visions and spectral connection to other places and times were at the hand of some *entity*.

Eliza.

Anna felt the name like a needle in her mind. With a shiver, her visions drifted to the tales whispered through time—tales of the witch named Eliza, who had forsaken the lands of France in 1685, crossing the treacherous ocean to seek dominion in the New World. The air shimmered around her, thick with Eliza's presence, and she knew she was not merely a spectator; she was trapped in the haunting reverie conjured by her predecessor.

As if summoned by Anna's presence, the vision of Eliza materialized before her—a figure clad in flowing garments that seemed to billow like smoke. The cold gleam of her emerald eyes pierced through the dark, and a wicked smile curled upon her young and sultry lips. "Welcome, my sister, Anna," she purred, her voice a silken caress laced with malice. "Let us take a journey into my past, shall we?"

Anna recoiled inwardly, but she was powerless to resist.

With a mere thought, Eliza propelled them through the veil of time, the world around them dissolving into a tapestry of swirling shadows and light until they landed upon a lonely shore, the salty air mingling with the scent of blood.

It was here, on the craggy coast of Maine in the past, that Eliza had made her mark. The year was 1685, and the village lay shrouded in darkness, the townsfolk oblivious to the terror that would soon descend upon them. Eliza surveyed the scene, her heart swelling with the anticipation of chaos. She could taste the power that surged through her, a symphony of fear and death that called to her like a lover's whisper.

"You see how easily they forget," she said, her voice echoing in Anna's mind. "They welcomed me as a healer, a woman of wisdom. But they did not know the darkness that brewed beneath my skin."

With a flick of her wrist, Eliza summoned shadows that twisted into grotesque forms, resembling the frightened villagers who would soon meet their fate. She felt the pulse of life within them, a heartbeat that quickened as they gathered in the town square, oblivious to the doom that awaited.

"Why did you do it?" Anna asked, her voice laced with both horror and fascination. "Why murder?"

Eliza's laughter rippled through the air like distant thunder. "Power, dear Anna. Power is the sweetest elixir. Each life I extinguished fed my essence, my very being. They were nothing but vessels for my will. With each soul I claimed, I felt the caress of my mistress, The Dark, guiding my hand."

The vision shifted, the town swirling into a tapestry of chaos. Anna watched helplessly as Eliza stalked through the night, a specter of death cloaked in shadows, leaving behind a trail of bodies—men, women, and children alike—each life violently snuffed out like a candle. The screams echoed in

Anna's ears, a cacophony that clawed at her sanity. Hundreds perished, their lives extinguished for Eliza's insatiable hunger, and a harvest reaped in the name of darkness. Legend would say that the high death toll was due to a lack of faith for the new colonizers, while some voices whispered of an unstoppable witch.

"You revel in their despair," Anna whispered, tears welling in her eyes. "You are a monster."

"Ah, but they named me a witch, a dark enchantress!" Eliza replied, spinning gracefully, her gown swirling like ink in water. "They feared me, and I found my power in that fear. Each name I was called, each curse hurled in my direction, only fed the hunger of The Dark. And I was never alone; the shadows danced with me."

The oppressive air thickened around Anna as she was suspended between realms, drawn inexorably into the dark embrace of Eliza's will. Time twisted like a serpent, coiling around her until she felt as if she were submerged in a dream—a nightmare woven from the very fabric of despair. The scene materialized before her: a quaint New England village bathed in the golden hues of dawn, heedless to the shadow that loomed just beyond its edges.

Eliza stood beside her, her presence palpable and darkly magnetic. "Look closely, Anna," she intoned, her voice a sultry whisper entwined with the echoes of ages past. Witness the birth of my legend in the New World."

As the villagers went about their morning routines, Anna felt an insidious chill creep through her, recognizing the fleeting innocence of those who had yet to taste the bitterness of dread. However, Eliza was a tempest, her hunger palpable, her desire for power thrumming in the air around them. Anna could not move; she was tethered to this moment, forced to observe as Eliza's malevolence unfolded.

In a flash, the village transformed from peace to chaos as Eliza weaved her destructive spell. She moved through the streets like a shadow incarnate, her chilling laughter echoing in the corners of every dwelling. One by one, the villagers began to succumb to her insidious influence—some falling to madness, others collapsing as their very lifeblood was drained.

"You see?" she said, her eyes gleaming with dark triumph. "Each life, a thread in the tapestry of my power. The Dark feeds upon their fear, their despair, and I am its hand."

Anna watched helplessly as the blood ran like rivulets through the cobbled streets, as parents wept for children and children cried for parents. The air became thick with the scent of smoke and iron, and with every scream, Eliza's laughter crescendoed, a symphony of chaos that drowned out the anguish surrounding them.

The scene shifted, the village now a charred ruin, the survivors haunted by grief and horror.

Anna felt the despair wash over her like a tide, but Eliza was unfazed, her countenance gleaming maliciously.

"And yet, the tale is not finished. Witness the folly of those who dare to challenge me," she said.

Instantly, they found themselves in another village, where the townsfolk, now armed with torches and pitchforks, sought to rid themselves of the witch they believed had cursed their lives. Eliza, unafraid, allowed herself to be captured, a mocking smile gracing her lips as they bound her to a stake, the flames licking at her feet.

"Foolish minions of a God that does not exist," she taunted, her voice reverberating above the crackling fire. "You think this can hold me?"

Anna's heart raced as the flames rose higher, devouring the wood and eating at Eliza's flesh. Was this moment what Anna had felt when she was shackled by Etienne?

Rather than scream or plead for mercy, Eliza began to chant—a low, sonorous incantation resonating with a power that shook the ground beneath their feet. The fire that consumed her began to shift, spiraling upwards as if under her command.

Anna gasped, realizing the true nature of Eliza's power. The flames transformed into orbs of molten fury, coalescing around Eliza, glowing brighter and brighter until they burst forth, raining down upon the villagers like wrathful meteors.

The crowd erupted into chaos, screams mingling with the crackling of fire as the fireballs struck with devastating force, igniting homes and bodies alike. Anna was forced to watch as the village was consumed, a pyre of destruction ignited by the flames seeking to destroy Eliza.

Eliza floated up, high and away from the chaos, by two large raven's wings that sprouted from her back. Unscathed by the flames, her laughter echoed through the air—a haunting melody of victory and madness. The remnants of the town lay smoldering beneath her, and she gazed down upon the surviving townspeople, her green eyes glowing with triumph, her black wings fanning the flames with their massive span.

"Look at what you have wrought!" she cried, her voice ringing with delight and incredible fury. "You sought to extinguish me, yet here I stand, a goddess of chaos, reborn in fire. Your fear nourishes me, and your grief grants me life!"

Anna's heart raced, torn between disgust and an eerie fascination. "You're a monster," she breathed, her power flickering weakly within her.

"A monster?" Eliza echoed, her laughter dripping with scorn. "I am a force of nature! Do you wish to understand the darkness, Anna? Then embrace it! Be the harbinger of your legend! Cast aside your hesitations and join me!"

As the scene began to dissolve, Anna felt a surge of energy—a choice hovering before her like a specter. Would she succumb to the same darkness that had claimed Eliza, or could she forge her own path amidst the ashes? Little did Anna know that it was impossible for two witches of their power to exist together for long. There could be only one servant of The Dark.

But the choice faded as Eliza's laughter echoed again, drowning out Anna's thoughts. The world turned black, leaving Anna trapped in her turmoil, ensnared by the shadow of the witch who had embraced the darkness and laughed at the flames.

Chapter Twenty Two

The chill mountain air, thin and sharp as shattered glass, bit at Anna's exposed skin as she then found herself ascending the treacherous slopes of Mount Parnassus in Greece. A place of unequaled mythology that she somehow had memories of. Why was she here? She knew where she was, like accessing a memory you thought long dormant. The twin peaks, shrouded in swirling mists like the breath of some slumbering titan, loomed above her, casting long, dark shadows that danced and writhed amongst the ancient olive groves. Anna, a novice in the arcane arts, a mere fledgling witch, had journeyed through time and space via her mortal death, drawn by whispers carried on the wind – whispers of Delphi, of the Oracle, of Pythia.

She had always felt a pull towards the unseen world, a yearning for the knowledge that lay hidden beneath the veil of reality. She had felt it her entire life and honed it after meeting the Chateau de Mornay—and Luc.

The ruins of Delphi, when she finally reached them, were a desolate spectacle of crumbling columns and shattered temples. Yet, even in their decay, they exuded an aura of ancient power, a palpable sense of the sacred. The air hummed with an almost imperceptible energy, a vibration that resonated deep within Anna's soul.

Next, she found herself at the adyton, the sacred chamber of the Oracle, nestled deep within the earth, a dark and cavernous space that smelled of damp stone and volcanic fumes. A faint, ethereal glow emanated from within, illuminating the swirling mists that clung to the walls like ghostly apparitions. And there, amidst the vapors, she saw her. Pythia. Not the withered crone of popular imagination, but a woman of ageless beauty, her face serene and ethereal, her eyes pools of ancient wisdom. She stood proudly, her form partially veiled by the rising fumes—and two giant black pythons with bright green eyes.

The Oracle's voice, when she spoke, was a low, resonant murmur that seemed to echo from the depths of time itself. "You seek knowledge, child," Pythia said, her gaze fixed upon Anna. "You seek to understand the nature of witchcraft, the duality that lies at its heart."

Anna, awestruck by the Oracle's presence, could only nod, her voice caught in her throat. For she knew this was her death she was witnessing. With any slight control she had, she chose to observe.

"Witches," Pythia continued, "are not simply beings of magic. They are vessels, conduits for forces both light and dark. There are those who wield their power for benevolent purposes, for healing and nurturing, for the preservation of balance and harmony. They are the guardians of the natural world, the keepers of ancient healing wisdom."

A vision bloomed before Anna's eyes: a verdant forest bathed in sunlight, where women with gentle hands tended to blooming herbs, their voices weaving incantations of healing and growth. She saw fields of golden wheat swaying in the breeze, blessed by whispered spells of abundance. She saw children laughing, their faces lit by the warm glow of hearth fires, protected by charms woven with love and care.

"These are the witches of the white path," Pythia explained. "They understand the interconnectedness of all things, the delicate balance between life and death, light and shadow. They wield their magic with respect and reverence, always mindful of the consequences of their actions."

But then, the vision shifted, darkening, twisting into a grotesque parody of its former beauty. The forest became a tangled thicket of thorns and shadows, the herbs withered and blackened, their scent acrid and poisonous. The fields of wheat turned to barren dust, the laughter of children replaced by wails of pain.

"And then," Pythia's voice dropped to a chilling deep whisper, "there are those who succumb to the allure of darkness, who wield their power for selfish gain, for vengeance and destruction. They are consumed by their own desires, blinded by their own ambition."

Anna saw images of women with faces contorted by malice, their hands clutching dark artifacts, their voices chanting curses that withered the land and poisoned the hearts of men. She saw storms raging without cause, crops failing, disease spreading like wildfire. She saw the light of hope extinguished, replaced by the cold, suffocating darkness of despair.

"These are the witches of the black path," Pythia said. "They seek to control, to dominate, to impose their will upon the world, regardless of the cost. They revel in chaos and destruction, feeding on the fear and suffering of others."

Anna felt a chill run down her spine, a profound sense of unease. She suddenly understood the duality that Pythia spoke of, the two faces of witchcraft, the constant struggle between light and darkness. It was classic and simple, as if the information had been uploaded into her being.

"The choice," Pythia said, her gaze piercing Anna's very soul, "is yours. Every witch must choose which path she will walk. There is no middle ground, no easy compromise.

You must choose between the light and the darkness, between good and evil."

The mists within the adyton began to swirl more rapidly, obscuring Pythia's form. Her voice, as it faded, echoed in Anna's ears like a solemn warning, "Beware, child. The path of darkness is seductive, its allure powerful. But those who succumb to its embrace are ultimately consumed by it, their souls forever lost in the shadows. Whichever path you choose, I will be your guide without judgment. For I am the most ancient of all the mortal conjurers. Mortals have come to me for millenia. Men and women looking for guidance on their path to the light or the dark. Kings and warriors, wizards and mages. Even warlocks and witches, as you might say. They all come here just as you have. Forsooth, you have sacrificed the greatest gift to Apollo—*your life*. This sacrifice gives you power beyond any on Earth. Use it for either hope or destruction, but never forget," Pythia hissed as she leaned forward, her face contorting into the beautiful visage of Eliza warped into utter psychosis, "there can exist only one. I now bid your exit."

And then, Pythia was gone, vanished into the swirling mists, leaving Anna alone in the echoing silence of the adyton. The weight of the Oracle's words pressed upon her, a heavy burden of responsibility. She knew now the profound choice that lay before her.

As she descended the slopes of Parnassus, the chill mountain air no longer felt merely cold, but charged with the weight of her newfound knowledge, the knowledge of the eternal struggle between the light and the darkness, a struggle that raged not only in the world around her, but within her own heart.

Anna had received a great gift—the knowledge of all grimoires and all conjurers before and after her, given to her from The Oracle of Delphi, Pythia.

Chapter Twenty Three

Zoe sat in Ralph's Diner, a greasy-spoon joint popular near the college, the steam rising from her mug of coffee in a comforting blur. It was always open, and she spent countless nights haunting it working on her thesis. She stared out the window, the world a distorted kaleidoscope of colors. Frowning, she tried to see what the source of the strange colors was. Her mind raced, replaying the horrors she had witnessed on the videotape. Eliza's transformation, the twisted rituals from the past, the unspeakable acts of sex and violence on the tape. It was a nightmare that refused to fade.

The television, a silent companion in her solitude, interrupted its normal programming. A news bulletin blared, its urgency cutting through the quiet of the diner. The screen showed a chaotic scene: the Orrville Sanitarium, engulfed in flames. A news anchor, her voice trembling, reported that few had survived while dozens had perished. The fire was far away, but it illuminated the sky with both natural and unnatural colors and swirls.

Zoe's heart pounded in her chest. Eliza, the source of so much horror, was free. She knew it was Eliza who had done it. She had to have done it. Then Zoe's heart almost exploded when she thought of Rachel. She instantly tried to ring her cell. It went directly to voicemail, which was not a good sign.

Zoe dashed from the diner to get to the burning sanitarium as fast as possible. Although Eliza was on her mind because of the danger of her running loose, Rachel was paramount in her thoughts. But from what she had just seen on the news, the sanitarium appeared as a war zone, aflame and crumbling, with white gowned patients wandering about, lost, injured, and being gathered by first responders. Zoe reached her car and opened the door.

As she did so, there was a whisper of a voice, a haunting melody that seemed to echo in the depths of her mind. It was a voice she recognized, a voice she had heard on the videotape.

"Come, Zoe," the voice whispered. "Join me in the darkness." The voice was childlike and full of evil delight. Zoe tried to shake it off, to dismiss it as a figment of her imagination. But the voice persisted, growing louder, more insistent. It was a siren song, a terrifying and irresistible temptation.

Her mind raced. She knew the danger. Eliza was a force of pure evil, a creature of darkness that threatened to consume everything in her path. But the voice, the call, was too powerful. It was a calling she could not resist.

Zoe closed the car door, her movements almost automatic, her mind a whirlwind of conflicting emotions. She knew she should run and seek help, but the voice, the call, was too strong:

Through fog-choked streets, her eyes gleam,
Eliza whispers, a haunting dream.
Come, little one, where shadows teem.

As she stood by the diner, the world around her seemed to blur. The sky was a canvas of swirling Picasso colors, the buildings a distorted mass of shapes.

The voice was louder now, and there was a constant, haunting hum in her ear. "Come to me," it whispered. "Join me for a cup of tea."

Zoe began to walk, her steps almost trance-like. She didn't know where she was going but knew she had to follow the voice. She was drawn to it without thought. The world around her faded, replaced by a vision of darkness. She saw someone in the road, a monstrous figure shrouded in shadow, eyes glowing with an unnatural green light. It was Eliza, beckoning her to join her in the abyss.

She turned around and ran, fighting every thread of control over her mind.

The voice followed Zoe, a constant nightmarish whisper in her ear. But she fought back, her mind a battleground of light and shadow. She was stronger than she thought, more resilient.

As she ran, the voice faded. The darkness that had consumed her began to dissipate. She was free, at least for now. But she knew that the battle was far from over. She stopped. Eliza was still out there, and she would not give up.

"No, I will not," Eliza's voice boomed directly behind Zoe. She swung around and wanted to scream upon seeing the ghastly witch only feet from her. Zoe froze, her body shivering from all her power to flee, squelched by Eliza's hold.

Eliza stepped so close to Zoe that the doctoral student felt the cold of her skin. It was like ice emitting a freezing wave that made her try to recoil yet fail. "I need you. I want to tell you my story," Eliza whispered in her raspy voice. "Come with me, child."

Zoe gave in and allowed Eliza to take her, controlling her body as they walked away. She was frightened to death, but somehow she believed that Eliza told the truth. The tear falling down her cheek said otherwise. She was ensnared by the witch and had likely been her pawn for some time.

Chapter Twenty Four

Darkness was her companion—a cold, oppressive void stretching infinitely. There was no sound, no sensation, only an overwhelming sense of nothingness. Yet, within this abyss, a flicker of consciousness emerged, a desperate yearning for light. Slowly, painfully, sensation returned—the weight of a cold, heavy metal against her chest, a searing pain that seemed to originate from her very core. Then, a blinding flash of light followed by a wave of nausea that threatened to consume her.

Anna's eyes fluttered open, and the world rushed in, a chaotic swirl of color and sound. She was alive. A scream tore from her throat, a sound born of both terror and disbelief. She had failed. The sword, still embedded in her chest, was a mocking testament to her folly.

The room was dim, illuminated by a single window casting grotesque shadows on the walls. The air was thick with the scent of decay, a stench that seemed to seep from the massive room's fabric. She was lying on the stone floor, cold and unforgiving. As her senses sharpened, she became aware of the body. Her body. It was wrong. Once porcelain smooth, her skin was now gray and translucent, veined with an unnatural blue. Her hair, once a cascade of yellow, was now a tangled mass of black. And her eyes, once filled with a passionate fire, were now cold and empty, the color of the Emerald City from Oz.

A sob escaped her lips, a sound filled with despair and rage. She had yearned for death, for eternity with Luc, and instead, she had been granted a curse far worse than death: immortality. Good or bad, she was immortal. She had met Eliza in her death. She had gathered powers beyond her imagination.

The sword, a relic from a forgotten age, pulsed with an unnatural energy. It was a weapon, yes, but it was also something more. A conduit, perhaps. A connection to a power she had unwittingly tapped into and caught Eliza's attention. A cold determination filled her. She would not be a victim. She would master this curse and use it for good, this transformation. If she could not join Luc in death, she would bring him to her, or at least his spirit. She would become more than a witch. She would become a necromancer, a mistress of life and death. It was all within her, the conflict of light and dark were waging inside her dead mortal body. With a superhuman effort, she pulled the sword from her chest. Dark and dense blood poured forth, but it seemed to invigorate instead of weaken her. The wound closed rapidly, leaving only a faint scar.

"It has happened then," Etienne said from behind her, his eyes witnessing the aging changes to her body. She was still tight and beautiful, but her skin was much greyer and had veiny cracks throughout.

Anna turned her naked body around to face Etienne and saw that he was fully clothed in his usual handsome attire. "What has happened to me?" she cried out, her monstrous appearance belying the gentle voice of her former self. Her hands tore at her black hair as she realized the color change for the first time. She was trapped. It was her worst nightmare, devoid of all independence and choice. Anna's screams filled the enormous room and reverberated between the black stones, never to leave the forlorn walls, trapped for eternity.

"You have become what you were meant to be, Anna," Etienne said. "Why do you think I made you suffer? It gave me no pleasure to do those things. But you must complete your transformation into a mistress of The Dark."

Tears poured from Anna's troubled eyes. "What do you know of The Dark, you weak phantom? I have seen it all! I know all! You know nothing compared to me!"

Etienne stumbled back at her uncharacteristic outburst. "It is the bringer of death to all things, even me, Anna. It has waged war against mankind since ancient times. It is unholy, yet I need it. I've waited for centuries to end this existence, where I am a slave to immortality. You will do this for me. I hastened the change in you. I cannot wait any longer. Anna, please end my suffering!"

Etienne kneeled before the naked Anna, his head bowed, hair hanging in his face. "Kill me, Anna. I've waited so long for this. Take me to God."

Chapter Twenty Five

The moon, a pale, ethereal orb, cast an otherworldly glow upon the ancient oak. Beneath its watchful gaze, two bare women entwined on soft green moss, their bodies a testament to the primal beauty of passion.

Eliza, the dark seductress, her skin as smooth as satin and her eyes the color of fresh lichen, was the first to move. Her fingers traced the delicate curves of Anna's back, her touch sending shivers down her spine. Eliza's hand slid down to Anna's bottom and she squeezed a handful. Her fingers then touched her heated wetness that was waiting for the dark witch's caress.

Anna's equally emerald witch eyes shimmered with desire. Her heart pounded with an unfamiliar intensity, even beyond anything she had felt with Luc, as she leaned into Eliza's touch. The dark seductress's fingers entered Anna's parted, soaked lips, pushing deep inside and touching the delicate spot where only the experienced traverse. Eliza's thumb pushed on Anna's black, prickly hair, then trickled down to her clitoris, where she rubbed gently. Anna's mouth parted, a soft, inviting sigh escaping her lips as Eliza used three fingers on her. Despite the ecstasy, Anna felt that her movements were not entirely hers. She cared not. Eliza's practiced motion was a sensation that no man had ever given her.

Luc's voice suddenly resounded in Anna's head. "Who is she?"

Eliza's gaze met Anna's, her eyes filled with an ancient and consuming hunger. She lowered her head slowly, her lips brushing against Anna's cheek, then her neck. Anna's breath quickened as Eliza's touch inside her vagina ignited a fire within her. Anna's eyes widened, and she let out a gentle, yet precise, orgasmic squeal.

With a trembling hand, Anna reached up, her fingers tangled in Eliza's perfect black hair. She pulled closer, her lips meeting Eliza's in a passionate kiss.

"This isn't right," Luc whispered in Anna's mind.

Eliza's tongue explored Anna's mouth, a dance of desire that was both sensual and intoxicating. Anna responded, her body trembling with the intensity of the moment. Eliza then guided Anna's hand onto her breasts and Anna squeezed them and played with her pink nipples. She slipped her entire hand over Eliza's black pubic hair and cupped her dripping wet, silky inner labia. Unlike Anna's gentle vocalizations, Eliza moaned madly, almost frightening Anna with her maniacal and unexpected volume.

"Don't do it! She feels dangerous!" Luc said in desperation.

Their bodies entwined, a symphony of flesh and blood. Eliza's hands moved with a practiced grace, tracing the contours of Anna's body. Anna's hands, trembling with anticipation, explored Eliza's, her touch gentle, yet firm.

"Anna! No!"

As their passion peaked, they surrendered to the moment, their bodies merging in a physical and spiritual union. The world around them faded, replaced by a universe of their own creation.

When the storm of their passion subsided, they lay entwined, their bodies bathed in the moonlight. Anna's eyes were closed, her breathing deep and even. Eliza watched her, a soft smile playing on her lips.

"You are so beautiful," Eliza whispered, her voice a caress against Anna's cheek, "like a goddess fallen from Olympus."

Anna opened her eyes, her gaze filled with a love that was both profound and eternal. "You are my world," she replied, whispering.

"She is not your world!" Luc bellowed, ignored by the spellbound Anna.

As they lay together, the moon watched over them, a silent witness to the power of their union. And in that moment, they knew that their bond was unbreakable.

Anna awoke, standing in the middle of the large main room of Marchessault Castle again. She opened her eyes, and they were as white as snow. Within moments, they returned to their new green coloring. After yet another dream or vision cast upon her by Eliza, Anna recalled where she was and lamented her new life. She was still naked, and her body had changed. She looked down and saw the wrinkles of an older woman as tears ran down her face.

Etienne kneeled before her. "Send me to God, Anna. I beg you."

Recalling the knowledge of light and dark that Pythia had granted her, Anna suddenly jolted, full of the energy that had flirted with her during her metamorphosis. A devilish smile crossed her face. She appeared as a mad woman as she reached toward Etienne's head, his eyes still cast toward the floor. She knew she could kill Etienne with a mere thought. All the power of the ancient coven coursed through her body. All the pain Etienne had caused Luc and his family, and now her under his tortuous reign. Every instinct told her to destroy him immediately. But what path would that be?

"Do it, Anna. I am ready," Etienne said with an uncharacteristic calmness amidst his desperation. "I've waited centuries."

Anna raised her hand in the air and began an ancient incantation. A blinding light filled the large room, and when it had dissipated, she stood beautiful again in a green gown trimmed with black that matched her emerald eyes, her raven hair brushed and shimmering. "Not yet, Etienne. There is more to come for you."

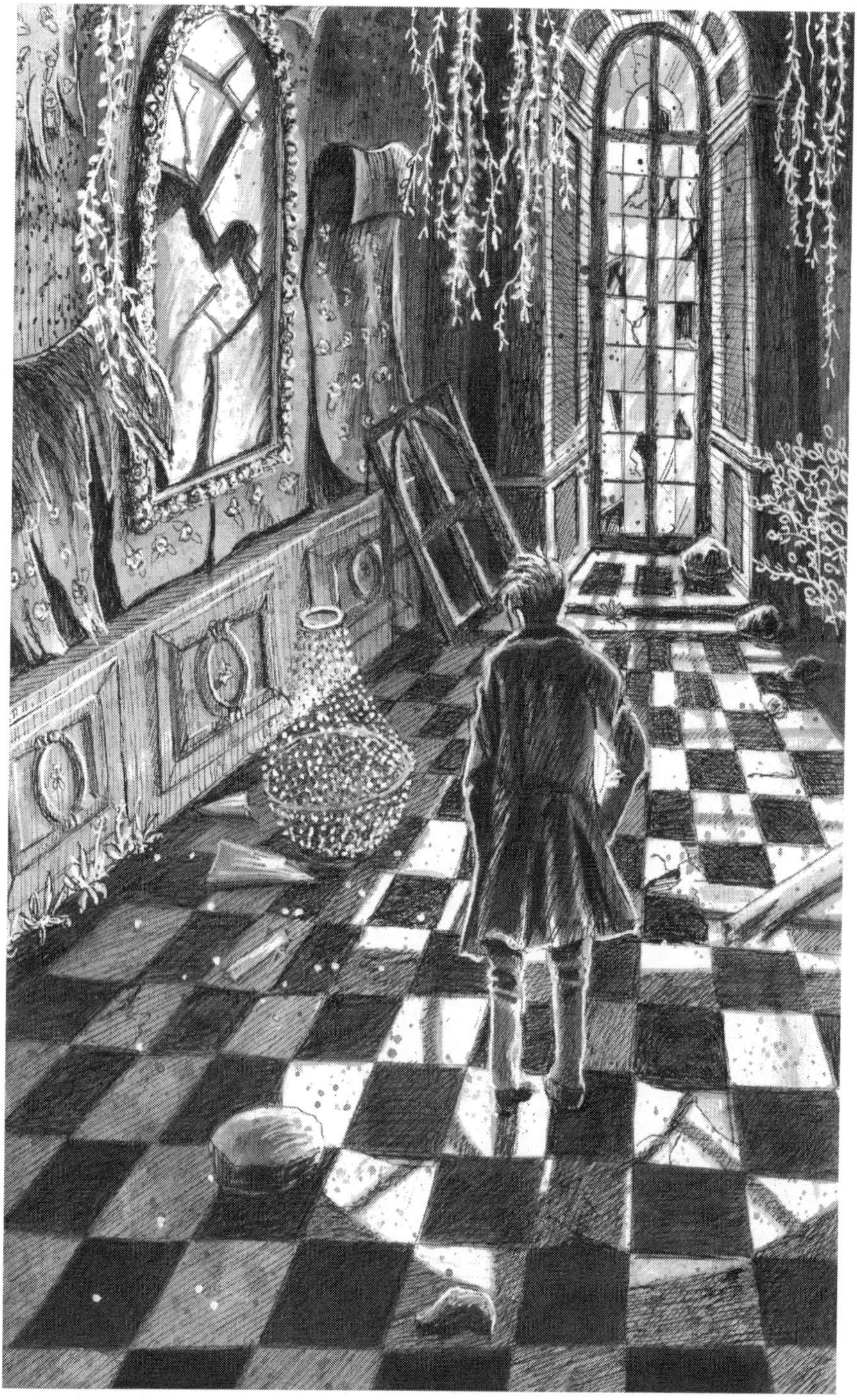

PART THREE

Chapter Twenty Six

The wind howled through the skeletal remains of the chateau, a mournful dirge that seemed to echo Bradley Stone's despair. He had returned, drawn by an inexplicable pull, a phantom hope that flickered amidst the ruins. But the sight before him was a stark, desolate truth: the chateau was no more.

A mere husk of blackened stone and twisted metal remained. Smoke still curled lazily from the remnants, a ghostly apparition in the twilight. It was as if the very essence of the place had been consumed by flame, leaving behind a void as chilling as the winter wind.

He had come back fragile and scarred, both physically and spiritually. The darkness that had assailed him within these walls had nearly consumed him. He bore the mental marks of its assault – livid scars of aging that marred his handsome face, a haunting emptiness in his eyes. Yet, the allure of Anna, the woman who had shared this dreadful place with him, had been too strong to resist.

Brad remembered the night of their arrival, a promise of a new beginning, a refuge from the dark world of grief, or so they had thought. But the chateau had held a sinister secret, a malignancy that had seeped into their lives. The thoughts of Anna's terror, her desperate pleas, echoed in his mind. And now this.

A bitter cold seeped into his bones as he wandered through the ruins. Where happiness and love once existed, there was now only silence and desolation. The chateau had claimed them both with its dark secrets and malignant presence. He was a survivor, yet he felt more like a ghost haunting the ruins of his own life.

As darkness enveloped the land, Brad stood amidst the wreckage, a solitary figure against the desolate backdrop. The wind whipped at him, a tangible reminder of the forces that had consumed his world. And as he gazed into the heart of the ruins, a cold dread settled upon him. For in the ashes of the chateau, he sensed a darkness more profound than any he had yet encountered.

As he wandered through the ruins, a figure emerged from the shadows, a man with a sharp nose and piercing eyes. He wore a black trenchcoat and fedora hat. "My name is inspector Boucher. I'm investigating the fire and possible death of Anna Stone. Who might you be?"

Brad extended his hand, and they shook. "I'm Bradley Stone. Anna is my wife. I've been looking for her and trying her cell. It goes straight to voicemail," he said, his voice trembling with emotion.

Boucher listened intently, his eyes never leaving Brad's face. "Were you having any marital issues? A fight, perhaps?

Brad decided to lie to get the inspector off his back. "I actually had to return to California for work several weeks ago. Something came up. I'm an actor."

Inspector Boucher squinted at Brad. "Yes! I've seen at least one of your films. Lots of action. Guns a blazin' like Clint Eastwood," he said while making motions with his hands as pistols. Boucher seemed skeptical, his gaze lingering on Brad's face. "So, you were in California the night of the fire two days ago?"

"Correct. And we had no issues. We had just moved in and were starting over from the loss of our young daughter," Brad said.

Boucher scribbled in his notepad. "I'm sorry for your loss. What was your daughter's name?"

Brad wanted the man gone. He wasn't ready for a line of questioning so soon after the fire. Audrey was another subject he didn't want to speak about. "Her name was Audrey. She died in a fall from a hotel in New York City."

"My condolences, Mr. Stone. Losing a child is hell for any parent."

"Thank you, Inspector."

"I know you haven't been in France for long, but did you have any enemies or acquaintances, possibly from here or America who would want to harm you or Anna?"

Brad put on a show. After all, it was his profession. He thought for a moment. "No. Anna is…was the sweetest woman I've ever known, and we have no enemies." Except whatever the fuck was inside that chateau, he thought.

Boucher's eyes narrowed. "You are sure there is no one who would want to harm you or your wife? This is a very suspicious case, Mr. Stone. Chateau de Mornay has stood for hundreds of years and many have tried to reduce it to ashes or rubble."

Brad hesitated for show, a flicker of doubt crossing his face. "I am certain," he said finally, his voice firm.

Boucher nodded, but his expression remained unconvinced. "Was Anna wearing any jewellery that could have been subject of a heist, or something that we can find in the ashes, if you beg my pardon?"

"Anna always wore a gold Cartier watch I gave her on our fifth anniversary," Brad said as he noticed another man sifting through the ashes, likely Boucher's partner or local constable from Corveau.

Boucher's expression remained unchanged. "What about the last time you talked or texted her on her cell?"

"It was two days ago. She sounded upset." Brad caught himself giving away too much. *Dammit!*

"What do you believe she was upset about, Mr. Stone?" Boucher asked as he continued scribbling in his notepad.

"It's hard to say. Her message was brief," Brad said.

"Would you mind if I listened to the message?" Boucher asked.

"Not at all," Brad replied. He pulled his cell phone out of his coat pocket, hit a few buttons and put in on speaker.

Anna's voice was clearly shaken. "Honey…I changed my mind…don't come here. It's dangerous for you, but I'm okay. I need to wrap up a few things, then I'll fly home to LA. Please. I beg you to stop as soon as you're at the next airport. Go home. I'll meet you there. Call me when you can. I love you."

Boucher nodded slightly. Anna's voice was hurried and panicked. He wrote more notes. "Dangerous? What do you think she meant?"

Brad lied again. "It was so sketchy with the renovations. Floors collapsed and jagged wood everywhere. She didn't want me hurt." He intentionally left out the conversation he and Anna had before she left the message—the one where she told him to come as fast as he could. It was best that the inspector didn't know all the information at this point. Brad was certain that Anna had perished, and he wanted the inspector gone and to be left alone.

Boucher looked over the remains of the chateau. "Dangerous renovations. Yes. Absolutely," he said in his above average English with only a slight French accent. "What will you do now? I expect that you'll stay in Corveau until this is sorted out?"

Brad rubbed his forehead in frustration. He was ready to walk away. "I don't know. I suppose I will," he said, his head beginning to throb. He handed Boucher a business card with his personal number on it. "Call me if you find her remains or anything else, such as her watch."

Boucher's expression was sympathetic as he shook Brad's hand. "Thank you for your time and cooperation, Mr. Stone. I'll inform you if we make any discoveries or have more questions. From my experience, I believe your suspicions are correct, and she did not survive the fire. If we find any identification such as the watch, I'll call you." He walked back from where he had appeared within the ruins of the chateau, leaving Brad alone with his thoughts and his grief.

As Brad stood amidst the wreckage, he felt a chill run down his spine. He had the feeling that Boucher was not convinced of his innocence, that he suspected him of being involved in Anna's disappearance. But Brad had nothing to hide. He wasn't even in the country at the time. And of course, he had loved Anna dearly, and he would never do anything to hurt her.

As the sun began to set, casting long shadows across the ruins, Brad turned and walked away from the chateau, his heart heavy with grief and uncertainty.

The village of Corveau was cloaked in a shroud of melancholy. Once a quaint, sleepy hamlet, it now seemed to share in the desolation that had consumed the chateau. As Brad stepped from the taxi, the familiar cobblestone streets, once filled with the chatter of villagers, were hushed and deserted.

Le Corveau Inn, the stone building with a weathered facade, was a stark reminder of happier times. They had stayed here, Anna and Brad, before their unfortunate decision to purchase the chateau. With a heavy heart, he entered the inn. The familiar scent of wood smoke hit him, a tangible phantom of the past, just like the old woman who greeted him the same as when they first arrived. She had a different countenance now. It was as if she knew what had happened to them and was now angry they didn't even try to listen to her non-verbal warning.

His room was unchanged. The same simple furnishings, the same view of the village square. It was as if time had stood still, waiting for their return. But they were not together. As the inspector had said, Anna was likely gone, consumed by the flames that had devoured their dreams. Although no body had been found, nor any remains, they suspected that she had burned, the inferno so intense as to leave nothing of her behind. If she had survived, where was she? Wouldn't she be here too, waiting for his return?

Days turned into nights as Brad retreated into a solitary world of grief. He spent his hours locked in the room, a prisoner of despair. The silence was deafening, a void that echoed the emptiness within him. Memories of Anna flooded his mind, a bittersweet torment. He recalled her laughter, her spirit, her courage. And then the horror, the fear, the finality that he would never see her again.

The shadows danced on the walls at night, grotesque caricatures of his despair. He would lie awake, listening to the wind howling outside, a mournful dirge that mirrored his sorrow. Once a haven of comfort, the room had become a mausoleum of memories.

The villagers whispered about him, their eyes filled with pity. They knew the story of the beautiful young couple and the tragic fate of the chateau. But their sympathy offered no solace when he ventured out for walks in town. Brad was alone in grief, a solitary figure adrift in a sea of despair. As the days passed, a sense of detachment began to creep over him. The world outside seemed distant, unreal. He existed in a twilight realm, a place where time had lost its meaning. And in the heart of this lonely existence, a cold, gnawing fear began to grow. For in the depths of his sorrow, he sensed a darkness, an evil presence that seemed to linger in the shadows.

It was a darkness that echoed the one that had haunted him in the chateau, a sinister force that threatened to consume him entirely.

Le Corveau Inn was a place of shadows and secrets. Its ancient walls seemed to whisper tales of the past, their echoes mingling with the mournful silence that enveloped Brad. He sat alone in his room, a solitary figure bathed in the dim glow of a single candle. A portrait of Anna, his beloved wife, perched above the fireplace. Her eyes, filled with a warmth that seemed to defy death, stared down at him. He had brought the portrait with him, a desperate attempt to hold onto a memory that was slipping away.

Days turned into a week. Brad's once-vibrant spirit withered, replaced by a profound melancholy. He spent his days wandering the empty halls of the inn, his footsteps echoing like the mournful cries of a lost soul.

At night, he would return to his room, haunted by the specter of his past. The Chateau de Mornay, once a place of love and laughter, now seemed like a nightmare. The darkness unleashed within its walls had followed him, a relentless shadow that taunted and tormented him.

The silence in the room was deafening. Every creak of the floorboards, every slight noise outside the window, amplified the emptiness that had become Brad's constant companion. Anna. The very air seemed to hold the ghost of her laughter, the faint scent of her favorite jasmine perfume still lingering in the bathroom days after.

A wave of grief washed over Brad, so intense it stole his breath away. He closed his eyes, trying to conjure her image, her smile, the way her eyes crinkled at the corners when she laughed.

But all he saw was darkness.

Each hour was a monotonous repetition of grief. He ate mechanically, slept fitfully, haunted by dreams where Anna was just out of reach, a fleeting shadow in the periphery of his vision.

He recalled one evening years ago, while sorting through a pile going to charity, he came across a small, intricately carved wooden box. He opened it carefully. Inside, nestled amongst its soft, velvet lining, lay a collection of tiny, pressed flowers. Each one was delicate, vibrant even in death, a testament to Anna's love for the natural world.

As he gently touched each fragile blossom, a memory surfaced. It was a summer afternoon, years ago, when they had gone for a picnic in the meadow near their home. Anna, ever the romantic, had spent the afternoon collecting wildflowers, weaving them into a makeshift crown for him. He remembered her laughter, the way the sunlight had caught in her hair, her eyes sparkling with joy.

Tears welled up in his eyes, but this time, they weren't tears of despair. They were tears of remembrance, a bittersweet acknowledgment of the love they had shared. He realized that while Anna was gone, her love remained. It lived in the echoes of her laughter, in the scent of jasmine, in the warmth of the sun on his skin.

He knew he would never forget Anna, that the ache of her absence would always linger. But he also knew that he had to live, to honor the life they had built together. He would carry her memory within him, a precious treasure to be cherished forever, next to Audrey.

He began to hear voices, whispers that carried on the wind like the cries of the damned. They spoke of Anna, her suffering, and the evil that had consumed her. The words were a poison seeping into his mind, twisting his thoughts. Brad could not imagine Anna in a place of pain.

One night, as he lay awake, staring at the photo, he felt a presence in the room. It was a cold, oppressive sensation, a chill that seemed to seep from the very walls. He tried to ignore it, to convince himself it was just a trick of the mind. But the feeling persisted, growing stronger with each passing moment.

Then he saw it. A shadow, a dark, amorphous shape that seemed to slither along the wall. It was a creature of pure darkness, a manifestation of the evil unleashed within the Chateau de Mornay.

The shadow snake approached the bed, its movements silent but menacing. Brad tried to scream, but no sound escaped his lips. The creature hovered over him, its eyes glowing green with a vicious intensity.

A surge of terror swept through Brad. He felt his mind unraveling, his sanity slipping away. The creature seemed to feed on his fear, growing larger and more menacing with each passing moment.

Then, a blinding light filled the room. The creature vanished, its shadow dissolving into nothingness. Brad collapsed, his body trembling with exhaustion. He had survived, but at a terrible cost. His mind was even more shattered, his sanity a fragile thing clinging to the edge of a precipice. The Dark had taken even more from him.

He was alone, haunted by the phantom of his past, a prisoner of his madness. The darkness that had consumed Anna had now claimed him, a victim of the evil unleashed within the Chateau de Mornay.

Chapter Twenty Seven

A shroud of fog choked the ancient forest, clinging to the skeletal branches like an unearthly garment. Zoe, the young woman with bright eyes and an unrelenting curiosity, pushed through the undergrowth, her boots sinking into the spongy earth. She followed Eliza helplessly. The air was thick with the scent of decaying leaves and something more primal, something that sent shivers down her spine. Eliza took no steps. She seemed to be floating above the boggy ground, her gown billowing hauntingly.

Moonlight, filtered through the dense canopy, illuminated a clearing ahead. In its center stood a weathered cottage, its thatched roof sagging like the back of a hunchbacked man. Smoke curled from its chimney, a thin, gray plume against the oppressive sky.

As Zoe and Eliza approached, the creaking of the rusted gate on its hinges seemed to pierce the suffocating silence. A moment later, the cottage door creaked open, revealing a woman of breathtaking beauty. Her raven hair, streaked with threads of silver, cascaded down her back like a waterfall. Her green eyes, the color of the borealis, held an ageless wisdom that sent a tremor of fear through Zoe. Eliza had changed, transformed into a remarkable beauty.

"But you were just there," Zoe said as she pointed near the door. The older version of Eliza that she had followed suddenly evaporated. Eliza had used bi-location, two places at once, something Zoe had heard rumors of. It was a power that only the most mastered in witchcraft could conjure.

As Eliza led Zoe into her cottage, the witch sang a haunting children's rhyme:

Eliza the witch, with eyes like the night,
Lives deep in the woods, where shadows alight.
Her laughter, a hiss, like a serpent's cold gleam,
She weaves wicked spells, a malevolent dream.
With toads as her pets and ravens as her spies,
She brews potions foul, beneath eerie skies.
She steals children's smiles, and their innocence too,
Leaving behind only shadows and rue.

Eliza stopped and stared awkwardly at Zoe. "You are the one who has been stirring the memories of forgotten nights." Her voice was a soft purr, like velvet brushing against raw silk.

Zoe, her throat constricting after hearing the dirge, managed a shaky nod. "I... I'm Zoe. I've been studying you for years."

A ghost of a smile played on Eliza's lips, an unsettling glimpse of something predatory beneath the surface. "Studying me?" she echoed, the word dripping with disdain. "These are not stories for prying eyes, child."

Emboldened by a foolhardy mix of curiosity and terror, Zoe stepped forward. "But they're important. Your story is important."

Eliza's smile vanished, replaced by a glacial stare. "My story is a tapestry woven with shadows and secrets. It is not meant for the likes of you."

Something cold slithered down Zoe's spine. The air crackled with a sudden unseen energy, and the whispering leaves outside seemed to sharpen into a chorus of accusations. "I came here to learn," Zoe pressed, her voice a fragile thread in the oppressive silence. "To understand."

A low chuckle escaped Eliza's lips, a sound devoid of warmth. "Understanding," she said, her voice a chilling whisper, "can be a terrible burden, child. One that can crush the unwary heart."

Nonplussed by the warning, Zoe produced a small tape recorder from her coat pocket. "I'm turning this on to record you. Please. I've been waiting so long for you. Tell me about the bodies buried on your property."

"Zoe," Eliza began, her voice a low, melodic whisper, "you wish to know the truth behind the bones, the remnants of lives extinguished long ago. I shall indulge your curiosity, though it may chill your heart and haunt your dreams."

Zoe leaned closer, the flickering light illuminating her pale skin. Her hair spilled over her shoulders like ink on parchment. "Please, Eliza," Zoe urged, "tell me your tale."

Eliza inhaled deeply, as though summoning the very essence of her past, and began to weave a narrative as twisted as the branches outside. "The villagers spoke in hushed tones of the witch who lived in the woods, but they did not know that I was more than mere superstition. I was a vessel for The Dark, a power that promised me salvation through sacrifice." Her voice dipped into a lower timbre, pulling Zoe into the depths of her memory. "I lured them with whispers of forbidden knowledge, with the promise of lost treasures hidden beneath the roots of ancient trees. They came to me, eager and unsuspecting, their hearts pounding with avarice and ambition, blind to their fate."

A shiver coursed through Zoe, the fire in the cottage crackling ominously as her words unfolded like a dark blossom.

"One by one, they crossed the threshold of my cottage, captivated by my charms. I welcomed them with a smile that masked the hunger within. Each offering—a man, a woman, a child—would bring forth a surge of power that coursed through my veins, igniting my spells and fueling my incantations. With their blood, I crafted the elixirs that deepened my bond with The Dark."

Her gaze shifted, distant, yet intense as if she had relived those moments. "The first was a farmer, his hands rough and calloused, his spirit imbued with the strength of the earth. He sought my aid to enrich his fields but found only his doom. I watched with fevered anticipation as I drew forth the vitality from his lifeblood, the essence of life feeding my dark ambitions."

"How could you do such a thing?" Zoe asked, her voice barely a whisper against the weight of her confession.

Eliza turned to Zoe, her eyes a storm of emotion. "Desperation makes monsters of us all, Zoe. In the shadows, I found solace, and in their pain, I found purpose. My power grew with each offering, as did my mistress's favor. But it was not enough. The Dark demands tribute, and I became a willing servant in a dance of shadows."

The room felt stifling, the air thick with the scent of burning herbs and old wood. "You spoke of many," Zoe pressed, dread knotting in her stomach. "What of the skeletons?"

"Ah, the skeletons," she mused, a cruel smile tugging at her lips. "They are the remnants of my artistry. Each bone is a testament to the lives I wove into the tapestry of my dark magic. Their spirits remained tethered to this world when their flesh was consumed, bound by the spells I cast. I needed them to feed The Dark with their essence, to sustain the power that thrummed within me."

A heavy silence enveloped them, punctuated only by the crackle of the fire. Zoe was paralyzed by the enormity of her deeds, by the chilling realization that the very ground beneath them was soaked in a history of betrayal and blood—and cannibalism. "Did you not feel remorse?" Zoe finally managed to ask, her voice trembling.

"Remorse is a luxury afforded to those who dwell in the light," she replied, her tone shifting to bitter nostalgia. "In darkness, I found strength. In their despair, I discovered liberation. But power is a fickle mistress, Zoe. It demands more than mere offerings; it craves devotion, and when I sought to break free from her grasp, she reminded me of my transgressions, of the blood that stains my hands."

As the shadows lengthened, the fire dimmed, casting the room into deeper darkness. Zoe felt the weight of Eliza's confession settling over her like a funeral pall, an inescapable truth that throbbed in the silence.

"Now you know," Eliza concluded, her voice a whisper lost in the crackling embers. "But the question remains—what will you do with this knowledge? Will you flee into the safety of the light, or will you embrace the darkness that lingers in us all?"

Zoe stared into the depths of the fire, grappling with Eliza's words, feeling the pull of the shadows around her. The choice lay heavy before her, a crossroads where morality and desire were entwined. As the night deepened, she felt The Dark's intoxicating lure—a tempting and treacherous whispering promise like the witch who had trapped her fate. Zoe, suddenly aware of the fact that she had Eliza Covington confessing to countless murders on an audiotape, felt a primal urge to flee. But before she could take a step back, Eliza extended a hand, her touch sending a jolt of icy fire through her veins.

Eliza took her hand and led her further into the cottage. Zoe felt in a daze and didn't know why she was there, as if her mind had been wiped. She dropped the tape recorder carelessly, and it thudded onto the wooden floor. Like a fading dream, her memory was restored to all her work studying Eliza. But the moment was brief, and she was interrupted by the witch's face, inches from her own.

Zoe felt Eliza's hot breath, which smelled of vanilla and cinnamon, two of Zoe's favorite scents. The air between their mouths turned briefly into a tiny mist and was suddenly within Zoe's lips. She breathed in and closed her eyes. That feeling. Love. There it was. She hadn't felt it in ages. Her work consumed her life, and she had flashes of it again. But the love in front of her, Eliza, with the flowing black hair and just enough gray to make it classy and intentional, looked suddenly ravishing to Zoe. A kiss on Eliza's lips made her smile, and Zoe caught what she wanted from Eliza.

Eliza licked Zoe's lips, slippery with their shared wetness. Her tongue entered Zoe's mouth, and Eliza squeezed her right breast. The shot of sexual energy that hit Zoe at that moment made her jump. She hadn't had sex in years and never before with a woman. She looked down and noticed that her clothes were different. She was wearing an old dress from hundreds of years ago. The confusion only lasted a moment as Eliza slid her hand up the dress and gently squeezed Zoe's lips through her panties.

"Do you enjoy how I touch you?" Eliza's voluptuous whisper was beyond intoxicating to Zoe. She had never been more aroused. Her first time with a woman. It was happening.

In the dim recesses of the cottage, whose very walls seemed to exhale the weight of centuries, Zoe leaned closer to the fire's dim glow as Eliza's fingers pulled her panties aside and entered her wet lips. The flickering light danced upon their features, casting shadows that twined and tangled with the ephemeral mists curling around them.

Zoe's heart raced with an uncertain mix of exhilaration and trepidation as she beheld the enigmatic Eliza, the witch of whispered lore and forbidden enchantments that she had studied for so long, rubbing her clitoris with her thumb as her middle finger slid in and out of her wetness. Zoe moaned and tossed her head back in ecstasy.

Eliza's presence was as arresting as the twilight itself. Her beauty, though otherworldly, bore an edge of antiquity—a haunting allure that bespoke of forgotten epochs and arcane secrets. Her eyes, deep and impenetrable as the abyss, held Zoe in their gaze. The witch's voice, when she spoke, was a melody that wove itself around Zoe's very soul, coaxing her into a state of intoxicating vulnerability. "You are so entrancing," she murmured, her words like velvet against Zoe's ear. "I have seen many, but none quite like you."

Zoe, the scholar, had embarked on her studies with the stern resolve of uncovering hidden truths in the darkness. Yet, as she stood in this forbidden chamber, her scholarly curiosity was eclipsed by Eliza's tangible, electric presence. The witch's caresses were gentle, a paradox to the dark allure she projected, and Zoe found herself lost in a haze of longing and surrender. Within moments, she orgasmed from Eliza's expert hand.

Eliza's wet fingers traced the line of Zoe's jaw with a delicacy that belied their strength.

Her touch sent shivers cascading through Zoe's body, an unfamiliar and intoxicating sensation. Zoe's breathing grew shallow, her rational thoughts dissolving into the fervent heat of the moment.

Eliza dragged her wet finger down to Zoe's mouth, and she sucked on it seductively. She thought she tasted her juices at first but then realized it was blood—her menstrual blood that Eliza had intentionally traced on Zoe's face in some kind of ritual. "Oh my God!" she yelled as she stepped back from Eliza. "How could you do that?"

Eliza only smiled and admired the bloody streaks on Zoe's face; streaks that tasted so good.

Then, in the throes of the witch's ritual, Zoe's eyes fell upon something ghastly amid the dim illumination. She turned her head, seeking to grasp reality amidst the overwhelming sensations that enveloped her. There, on a table within the scattered relics of the cabin's past, lay a mangled, rotting, decapitated human head, its remaining skin and facial structure that of the lost teenage girl. Teeth pulled and most of the hair removed, the bloody sight was so hideous Zoe recoiled, her pulse quickening as her rational mind grasped at the horrifying truth: Eliza had boiled the head and peeled off pieces of the face, possibly to eat. "Eliza!" she gasped, her voice a mere tremor of fear and disbelief. Her heart pounded as she attempted to distance herself from the grotesque sight.

The witch's eyes narrowed, the enchantment in her gaze shifting to a steely coldness. With a flick of her wrist, the cabin's atmosphere thickened with a palpable force, as if the shadows were gathering to enact her will. Zoe's flight was futile; the walls seemed to close in, and the oppressive gloom constricted around her like a living entity.

Before she could escape, Eliza's will was enacted with ruthless precision. The air crackled with an eerie energy, and Zoe was engulfed in an invisible force that halted her mid-step. Panic-stricken and desperate, her eyes widened with terror as she turned to face her assailant once more.

Eliza's features were now etched with an expression of cold resolve, her beauty stripped of its previous allure. Electricity and power glowed in her green eyes. In an instant, the witch's power was unleashed.

Zoe's breath was stilled, and her body stiffened as the spells took hold of her. Her final sight was of Eliza standing before her with a dagger. She was frozen as the dagger slowly approached her left eye, aware of it all but stiff as a board as the knife moved even closer. She felt the tip of the blade on her eyeball, then intense pressure, followed by unbelievable pain as the blade impaled her.

Eliza moved the dagger and pried the eye out as Zoe stood motionless, her screams muffled by the spell of imprisonment that the witch had conjured for her.

As her left eye hung down her cheek, Eliza grabbed the tendons holding it and severed the eye like cutting through a child's umbilical cord. Again, Zoe felt it all but could emit no sound.

Eliza repeated the process on Zoe's right eye, collecting her remaining one for more evil deeds. The pain Zoe endured was beyond anything she could ever imagine. Blood poured from her raw eye sockets as the tendons hung against her bloody cheeks.

"Don't worry, my child, "Eliza howled, "They will dry up and fall off exactly like a baby's cord." She flicked her wrist, and the holding spell on Zoe's subsided.

Zoe grabbed at her face, feeling the holes where her eyes used to be, screaming in terror and pain.

"I took your eyes because you have seen too much of me. You know more than you have earned. Now, your tongue so that your gossip about me will cease."

Zoe screamed as Eliza ignored a spell this time, grabbing her victim by the mouth, sliding her dagger inside, and cutting as she went deeper. Zoe screamed more, but only gurgling blood emerged from her mouth rather than words attempting to stop the mutilation.

Eliza let go and withdrew the dagger from her mouth, Zoe's tongue skewered on it grotesquely.

"Now for your ears because you have also heard too much." Eliza pounced, and the dull dagger cut through the base of her right ear until it was in Eliza's hand. She dropped it to the floor along with the eyes and tongue.

Zoe continued screaming, but the shock was setting in from the intense pain. She began to wobble.

"Oh, we're almost done, child," Eliza said in a motherly tone as she held Zoe up and sawed off her left ear. "Cutting these from you while alive gives them far more power in my spells than if you were dead. Thank you."

With that, Zoe collapsed to the ground, blood pooling crimson around her mutilated head. Her breathing slowed and then stopped.

Yet, even in death, the cabin's oppressive atmosphere seemed to pulse with a relentless rhythm, a testament to Eliza's dominion over life and death.

But death, in this place of ancient sorcery, was but a transient state. Eliza's incantation wove through the ether, and the once-mortal Zoe's body twitched and shuddered as the witch's dark arts reanimated it. The fire's glow cast grotesque reflections upon Zoe's newly lifeless, bloody face, which now held two tendons hanging from her eye sockets, blood pouring profusely from her missing tongue, and blood cascading down the open sided head wounds where her ears had been.

The reanimated Zoe rose, her movements jerky and unnatural, a marionette of Eliza's evil will. The witch watched with a cruel satisfaction as the soul that had once been vibrant and full of life now moved under her command—a puppet to her whims.

Eliza approached her creation, a grim, triumphant smile upon her lips. "Welcome back, my dear Zoe. In life, you were curious and bright; in death, you shall serve as a testament to the powers that transcend mortal bounds."

Eliza knelt and collected the eyes, tongue, and ears of her victim. She walked over to a misty large cauldron and dropped the bloody bits into it like she was making a stew.

The cottage's shadows seemed to close in tighter, and the room, once filled with passion, now harbored a more insidious dread. The witch's enchantments had wrought their cruel magic, transforming love and fear into a dark, unending reality.

It was then that Eliza knelt before Zoe, who lifted her gown, revealing her vagina with a little fur above it. Eliza pulled a chair over and placed Zoe's right leg on the seat, widening her lips. She moved in and kissed them, then began licking aggressively like a greedy pig at a trough. Zoe's face continued bleeding, and it stained her gown. Red trickles made their way down to Eliza's face as she was buried in Zoe's fur. The blood ran down and intermixed with Zoe's wetness. Eliza moaned with a devious smile of utter satisfaction from sexual pleasure and yet another successful necromancy—and necrophilia.

With her mouth buried in Zoe's dead vagina, Eliza finished her song, blood mixing with saliva and other juices on her lips:

So heed my advice, and stay far from her lair,
For Eliza the witch, delights in despair.
Her curses will bind, and your soul she will claim,
A victim of darkness, forever in shame.

Chapter Twenty Eight

Luc's love for Anna was a constant torment. He had watched her transformation with a mixture of horror and fascination. He had seen her embrace of the supernatural. And yet, his love for her had not wavered. He yearned to be with her, to share in her eternal existence.

In the dreamworld, he was finally reunited with her. They danced alone, their bodies moving in perfect harmony. Their laughter echoed through the empty ballroom of Chateau de Mornay, a joyous melody that seemed to defy the darkness surrounding them. The ballroom where so much death had occurred.

Suddenly the ballroom burst with light, and they were surrounded by revelers from one of the chateau's balls. Stringed music blared over the cacophony of mirth and conversations. Bell dresses whooshed along the floor, sweeping air like a fan in the hot room full of dozens of warm bodies.

Luc knew that the transformed ballroom was Anna's doing, as her new powers allowed her to adjust the dreamworld to her liking.

She stared into Luc's piercing blue eyes with an unmatched love. "I cannot die, Luc. I tried. I want to be with you forever. I want to bring you back," she whispered, her voice barely audible over the soft strains of the string music and laughter. "I want to free you from this eternal torment. I know how."

Luc's heart ached with a bittersweet longing. He knew the dangers of such a feat. To bring a spirit back to life was to tamper with the natural order of things, to invite the wrath of the uncontrollable supernatural. But it was Anna, his beautiful Anna.

"I would do anything for you, mon amour," he replied, his voice filled with a deep, unwavering devotion.

As they danced, Anna's power began to surge. A faint glow emanated from her body, a beacon of light in the darkness. The chateau seemed to respond, its ancient walls trembling with an unseen force.

Luc felt a surge of hope. Perhaps it was possible for him to be freed from his eternal prison, even deeper now that he existed only in a dreamworld.

As the dance reached its climax, Anna's power reached its peak. A blinding light filled the ballroom, and Luc felt a surge of energy course through his body. He was one step closer to life, a phantom once again, not just a vision inside a dream. Yet he was more than before—even with Anna's love that brought him back the first time. Luc felt stronger than ever. His second resurrection brought more power that he had to learn to use.

As the light faded, Anna's form began to shimmer around the throng of dancers. Her body seemed to dissolve, her spirit fading into the darkness. Luc reached out, his fingers grasping at empty air. "Anna!" he cried, his voice filled with despair.

But she was gone, a phantom of moonlight that vanished into the night.

Luc was free but at a terrible price. He was reunited with his love, but he had lost her yet again.

Chapter Twenty Nine

The slopes of Parnassus, a verdant embrace,
Where Delphi resides, in this sacred space.
But shadows now darken, a serpent's foul deed,
Pythia, the prophetess, lies bound and decreed.
By Python, the monster, with scales of dread gleam,
He guards the oracle, a venomous stream.
The air thick with poison, the ground stained with blight,
The voice of Apollo, is silenced in night.
But vengeance shall rise, on wings of the sun,
The god of the bow, his radiant course begun.
With arrows of gold, and a quiver so bright,
He descends on the mountain, a vision of light.
The serpents, they coil, with hissing so dread,
But Apollo, unyielding, with arrows ahead.
The first finds its mark, the second, the third,
The monstrous coils writhe, by the arrows interred.
The poison, it thickens, the air fills with pain,
Yet Apollo stands firm, amidst the foul rain.
With finality swift, the last arrow takes flight,
And Python, defeated, succumbs to the night.
The air is now cleansed, the shadows retreat,
The voice of the oracle, once more finds its seat.
Apollo triumphant, the victor proclaimed,
Delphi, his domain, forever unblamed.
He purifies the ground, with waters so pure,
And founds the great temple, forever secure.
Where wisdom shall flow, and prophecies gleam,
A beacon of truth, by the sun's golden stream.

The oppressive stillness of the adyton clung to Anna like a shroud as the song wrapped around her in a warming cloud, beautiful young voices singing, their story of Apollo strong and pure.

The familiar scent of volcanic fumes, once imbued with a sense of ancient mystery, now choked her, a constant reminder of her transgression. She had returned to Delphi, not as a seeker of wisdom, but as a supplicant, a penitent before the stern gaze of Pythia. The mists within the cavern swirled with an unnatural intensity, reflecting the turmoil within her soul.

Pythia sat upon her tripod, her ageless face etched with a sorrow that mirrored Anna's own. The ethereal glow that had once surrounded her seemed dimmed, replaced by a cold, eerie light.

Anna knelt before the Oracle, her head bowed, shame burning in her cheeks. She could not meet Pythia's gaze. The memory of Luc, his vibrant eyes, the warmth of his hand in hers, was now a poisoned chalice, a constant reminder of her desperate act.

"You have returned, child." Pythia's voice echoed through the cavern, devoid of the gentle cadence Anna remembered. It was a voice of cold pronouncements, a voice that carried the weight of ages.

Anna could only manage a choked whisper, "I... I have."

"You sought knowledge," Pythia continued, "and I showed you the two paths of witchcraft, the light and the dark. I warned you of the seductive allure of the shadows, the peril of succumbing to their embrace."

Anna's breath hitched. She knew what was coming. The truth, stark and unavoidable, hung heavy in the air between them.

"You chose the black path, Anna."

The words struck her like a physical blow. She flinched, a sob escaping her lips.

"I... I didn't mean to," she stammered, her voice trembling. "I only... I only wanted him back."

The image of Luc flashed before her eyes. The unbearable grief, the crushing weight of loss, had driven her to desperation. She had whispered incantations that chilled her to the bone. All in a desperate attempt to defy the natural order, to wrench Luc back from the clutches of death.

"You sought to usurp the power of the gods," Pythia's voice was laced with disappointment. "You believed you could cheat death, that you could control the very forces that govern life and death. That is hubris and foolhardy.

"I love him," Anna pleaded, tears streaming down her face. "I love him so much."

"Love is a powerful force, child," Pythia acknowledged, her voice softening slightly. "But love cannot justify transgression. Love cannot excuse the violation of the natural laws."

A vision unfurled before Anna's eyes, a horrifying tapestry of her dark magic. She saw herself, cloaked in shadows, chanting incantations under the baleful gaze of the moon. She saw the earth tremble, and the air grow heavy with a malevolent energy. She saw Luc's lifeless form stir, his eyes opening, not with the light of life, but with a cold, unholy gleam.

Anna recoiled from the vision, a cry of horror escaping her lips. She understood now the true cost of her transgression. She had not only brought back her beloved Luc; she had unleashed something terrible upon the world—herself.

"You sought to bring back life," Pythia said, her voice grave. "In your desperation, you have not only damned yourself, but you have also inflicted a terrible curse upon the mortals."

Anna's heart ached with a pain far greater than the grief she had felt at Luc's death. The weight of her actions, the terrible consequences of her dark magic, pressed down on her, suffocating her.

"What...what can I do?" she whispered, her voice barely audible.

Pythia's gaze pierced her, cold and unwavering. "The path you have chosen is a difficult one, child. Redemption is not easily won. You must undo the damage you have wrought, you must sever the connection you have forged with the dark forces. The path ahead will be fraught with peril, and you may not succeed. But you must try. For the sake of the world, and for the sake of your own soul."

The mists within the adyton swirled again, obscuring Pythia's form. Her voice, as it faded, was a somber echo, a constant reminder of her transgression.

"The choice, even now, remains yours. But know this, Anna: the darkness never truly relinquishes its hold. The scars of your transgression will remain, a constant reminder of the price of your desperate act."

And then, she was alone again, the oppressive silence of the adyton amplifying the weight of her guilt, the terrible knowledge that in her desperate attempt to reclaim love, she had instead embraced the darkness, and in doing so, had irrevocably altered her fate.

Chapter Thirty

The dim light of dawn seeped through the heavy tapestries of Marchessault Castle, casting somber patterns upon the cold stone walls. The castle, brooding and ancient, stood amidst the encroaching mists of early morning, its silhouette a monument to the ancient grandeur of its erstwhile inhabitants.

Within its chambers, Anna stirred from a fitful slumber, her heart still pounding with the echoes of a dream wrought with fiery magic.

She awoke in the opulent chamber that had become her refuge—a room adorned with rich velvets and gilded carvings, now draped in melancholy. The remnants of her nocturnal enchantment lingered in the air like a delicate fog, and as she sat up, her fingers traced the cool, black satin-clad sheets with a tremor of lingering energy. The memory of bringing Luc back as a spirit, of their entwined souls crossing the divide of life and death, was still vivid in her mind, its intensity almost tangible.

And then, there he was! Luc floated from the ceiling as real as ever with his shirt billowing and long auburn hair pushed by a supernatural breeze. "Mon amour," he said with such love in his eyes.

Anna beamed a smile. She had rescued him, and they could now live forever like this. "Come to my bed," she said, lifting the satin sheets next to her.

Luc descended to the spot, but before he reached it, he evaporated.

"No!" Anna screamed, a mighty scream that shook the very walls of Marchessault Castle.

But as Luc's brilliance faded, the weight of her reality descended upon her. The castle's heavy yet hauntingly beautiful air felt charged with a looming dread. Her breath came in shallow bursts as she tried to dispel the ethereal remnants of her vision of Luc and the hope of them coupling.

Then she heard the unmistakable sound of shuffling feet and a muffled, yet unmistakable, clang of metal upon stone. A thrill of unease shot through her, mingled with a surge of determination.

She hastened to the window, pushing the drapes aside to peer into the castle grounds. The morning mist hung low, obscuring her view, but she could see the silhouette of Luc's spirit form moving restlessly about the courtyard. Her heart quickened, a premonition gnawing at her. She did not doubt that the recent disturbances would attract unwanted attention—Etienne's, in particular.

A fierce storm of anger and betrayal had been brewing, and as if summoned by Anna's thoughts, the figure of Etienne Marchessault materialized from the fog. He looked every inch the vengeful spirit of a bygone era. His eyes, dark and turbulent as a storm, locked onto Luc with a fury that transcended even death.

Etienne's rage was palpable, an ancient vendetta that had simmered in the recesses of his being. The once-mortal friend of Luc, now a spirit of formidable wrath, had been drawn to the duel by the very force of Luc's resurrection. His form crackled with a menacing resolve as he drew forth a sword, its blade gleaming with an otherworldly sheen.

Luc's spirit form exuded an aura of faint luminescence. The glow of his form cast ghostly reflections upon the ancient stones of the courtyard, adding beauty to the scene. The once-clear lines of his visage were now softened and somewhat ethereal, but his blue eyes, never lacking the physical substance they once had, remained stubborn and unyielding as he stared down Etienne.

The two spirits regarded each other with mutual hostility and resigned acceptance. Etienne's voice, hollow and resonant, sliced through the morning air. "So, the flame of my foe is rekindled. Do you think, Luc, that your return will undo the ruin you wrought?"

Luc's response came with a calm that belied the turmoil of his soul. "Old friend, today you will die for your murderous ways."

Etienne stared down his adversary of centuries. He knew just as Luc did that their duel was mere folly and that neither could be injured, let alone killed. "Your anger is a shadow of a past that cannot be altered. But if you seek retribution, let us settle our score in this realm of spirits."

With that, he lunged forward swiftly, his sword slicing through the mists with a shimmering arc. Luc, moving with the fluid grace of a master swordsman, countered with an equally elegant parry, their shadowy weapons clashing in a duel that transcended mortal limitations. Their blades meeting echoed like distant thunder, a symphony of discord and defiance.

Luc moved with new confidence, having only encountered a sword in combat once while living—the night of his death. In this resurrection, he was an astute swordsman, possibly on the level of Etienne.

Anna, now dressed in dark black robes that matched her hair, watched from the shadowed archway of the castle, her heart gripped by a fierce urgency. The sight of the two spirits locked in their ghostly combat was a warning of peril and a grim testament to the power struggles that defined their dark existence. Her hands clenched into fists as she struggled to control the tumult of her emotions, her concern for Luc mingling with a sense of helplessness. She knew she could affect the duel's outcome with only a snap of her finger, but she wanted Luc to have his fun with Etienne first.

The courtyard became a battlefield of shadows and light as the duel raged. Each clash of their blades sent supernatural ripples and ghostly sparks through the mists, their combat painting a dramatic image upon the canvas of the morning fog. The forces of their will and wrath were palpable, their movements a blend of grace and ferocity that defied the bounds of their insubstantial forms.

Luc's attacks were relentless, fueled by his long-nurtured desire for vengeance—this foe had killed his family. He moved with a swiftness that seemed almost unnatural, his sword striking with a precision that spoke of countless battles fought and lost, which he had never experienced.

Etienne, in turn, defended with a resolve forged in the fires of his past, each parry and riposte a testament to his enduring spirit. His face a mask of cruel amusement, moved with the fluid grace of a panther. His sword, a wickedly curved rapier, sang a chilling melody as it found purchase in the air.

Luc, his auburn hair a halo against the mist, fought with a newfound ferocity. Resurrected, he possessed a strange, unnatural speed, his movements a blur of motion.

Yet, Etienne was a master swordsman, his years of service in France's wars evident in every parry, every riposte.

Luc, driven by intense rage, lunged, his sword a flash of silver.

Etienne, with a sardonic grin, sidestepped, the blade brushing past his rival's cheek, leaving an icy trail. He countered, his rapier a venomous snake, seeking its mark.

Luc, his eyes blazing with an unnatural light, deflected the blow, his own sword finding a weak spot in Etienne's guard.

The clash of steel echoed through the courtyard, a din of death.

Luc, fueled by his newfound power, began to press home the advantage. He moved with an uncanny agility, his sword a whirlwind of motion, forcing Etienne to retreat.

But Etienne, a cunning predator, bided his time, waiting for the slightest opening.

The duel reached a crescendo as the two spirits clashed in a final, thunderous convergence. The courtyard was bathed in a blinding light as their weapons met with a force that seemed to tear at the very fabric of the ghostly plane. The ground trembled, and a fierce wind swept through the castle, scattering the morning mist in a dramatic swirl.

As the blinding light receded, Etienne's shape wavered, his form dimming. "Yes! Finish me, witch!" he yelled out, knowing that the power was not Luc's doing. With a final, anguished cry, he fell back, his form dissipating into the fog as the last remnant of his rage was extinguished.

Luc stood victorious, yet bewildered, his form now dimmed but resolute. The duel, though concluded, left a somber silence in its wake, a testament to the depth of their hostility and the toll it had taken.

Anna stepped forward, her heart heavy with the weight of the conflict that had unfolded, her arms outstretched toward where Etienne had stood. Her gaze met Luc's, and in that moment, the tumultuous emotions of the duel gave way to a fragile silence. Now scarred by the duel's aftermath, the castle seemed to breathe mournfully.

"What did you do?" Luc asked Anna, her arms back to her side.

"I grew bored of you two wasting time trying to kill each other. You couldn't do it. So, I interceded. There's no way you could have beaten him. But, it was Etienne's time to die, and he knew it. He has been raising my power to end him. He has ascended to either Heaven or Hell, whichever his actions have decided."

Luc's form, though victorious, bore the marks of the battle, and as he approached Anna, an air of melancholy mingled with the triumph. "His storm has passed," he said softly, his voice a whisper of echoing shadows. But the battles we face are far from over."

Anna nodded, her eyes reflecting the solemnity of the moment. The castle, once a place of pain for her, now stood as a monument to the struggles ahead. The darkness that had marked their past was now a part of their present, and the path forward was fraught with challenges yet to be faced.

As the first light of dawn filtered through the castle's ancient windows, Anna and Luc faced the uncertain future together, bound by the trials they had endured and the shadows that still loomed. In the duel's wake, their weary spirits remained unyielding—a testament to their intertwined destinies' enduring struggle between light and darkness.

"I need to do something before I go," Anna said.

Luc admired her with his sapphire eyes and flowing auburn hair. Although she had become something very dark, he knew there was still love in her heart for him.

Anna looked at the towering black Marchessault Castle and opened her emerald eyes wide. A green fire blasted forth, hitting the stone of the castle wall and imploding it instantly. It began to fall like a child kicking a stack of rocks. The ancient building had stood for nearly a millennia but could not withstand the force of Anna's rage. Black rocks cascaded down upon them; Luc and Anna protected by a dark force that flung the rocks away. Luc watched, bewildered by Anna's new abilities and frozen by how she had used them to destroy him in Chateau de Mornay.

Green energy continued blasting from Anna's eyes, tearing through the castle with unnatural ease until the shadows cast by the structure were no more. Shadows that had stood for hundreds of years suddenly gave way to sunlight. The omnipresent mist around the castle, too, disappeared. It wasn't long before all that was left of Marchessault Castle was a dusty heap of broken rock.

Luc felt something toward Anna that he had never experienced: fear. Even in his last moments at the chateau, his confidence in taking from Anna what he desired had exceeded any other emotions. He had wanted her power just as Etienne had. But he wanted it no more now. Luc wanted Anna, even the new version of her.

Chapter Thirty One

The wick burns low, a ghostly gleam,
Then shadows rise, a silent scream,
And naught remains, in endless dream.

Now full and languid, the moon cast its eerie light across the land, weaving silver threads through the shadows of the craggy landscape. The earth, still shuddering from the ruin of Marchessault Castle, seemed to heave with an almost sentient agitation as though the crumbling stones had awakened something primal and deep.

Eliza, the dark witch who had ruled from the abyss of her somber domain, stood upon a jagged precipice near her old cave overlooking the remnants of the once-grand castle. Her keen eyes, dark green like the ink-stained skies, observed the tumultuous scene with a mixture of dark fascination and simmering ire. Anna's surge in power in resurrecting Luc and destroying Etienne and his castle had brought Eliza's terrible form back to the region for the first time in hundreds of years.

But it was only that - a unearthly bi-location. The real Eliza stood motionless in her cottage across the ocean.

Overlooking the castle's ruins, the witch's gown, a flowing cascade of sable silk, billowed about her in a gust of wind as she raised her arms to the heavens. A circle of eldritch runes blazed in a luminescent emerald beneath her feet, their power humming like a living pulse. Eliza's thoughts were dark and restless, consumed by the arrival of Anna—a new contender in the realm of shadow.

Anna, a fledgling witch with a spark of audacious power, had risen from the dust of her second brutal act, a feat which had made the ancient crone's blood run cold. The new witch had dared to transmute the ruin of Marchessault Castle into the stage of her grand sorcery, using its demise as a dramatic overture.

It was the recent, bold resurrection that troubled Eliza most—Anna's illicit achievement of reviving Luc, her slain lover, as a spirit stronger than he was before. Luc's return was no mere conjuration of the afterlife but a bold defiance of death's dominion. This act signaled a formidable surge in Anna's powers—a harbinger of an emerging rival capable of unsettling the equilibrium of their dark world.

With a deft wave of her hand, Eliza summoned her luminous raven from the shadows of her cave, its eyes glowing with an otherworldly fire. The bird's wings beat furiously as it circled above her, its cry piercing through the night's silence. The raven was her familiar, an extension of her will and a vessel of her far-reaching influence. It was corporeal and present as it swooped low and landed upon her outstretched disembodied arm, its ebony feathers shimmering like liquid midnight.

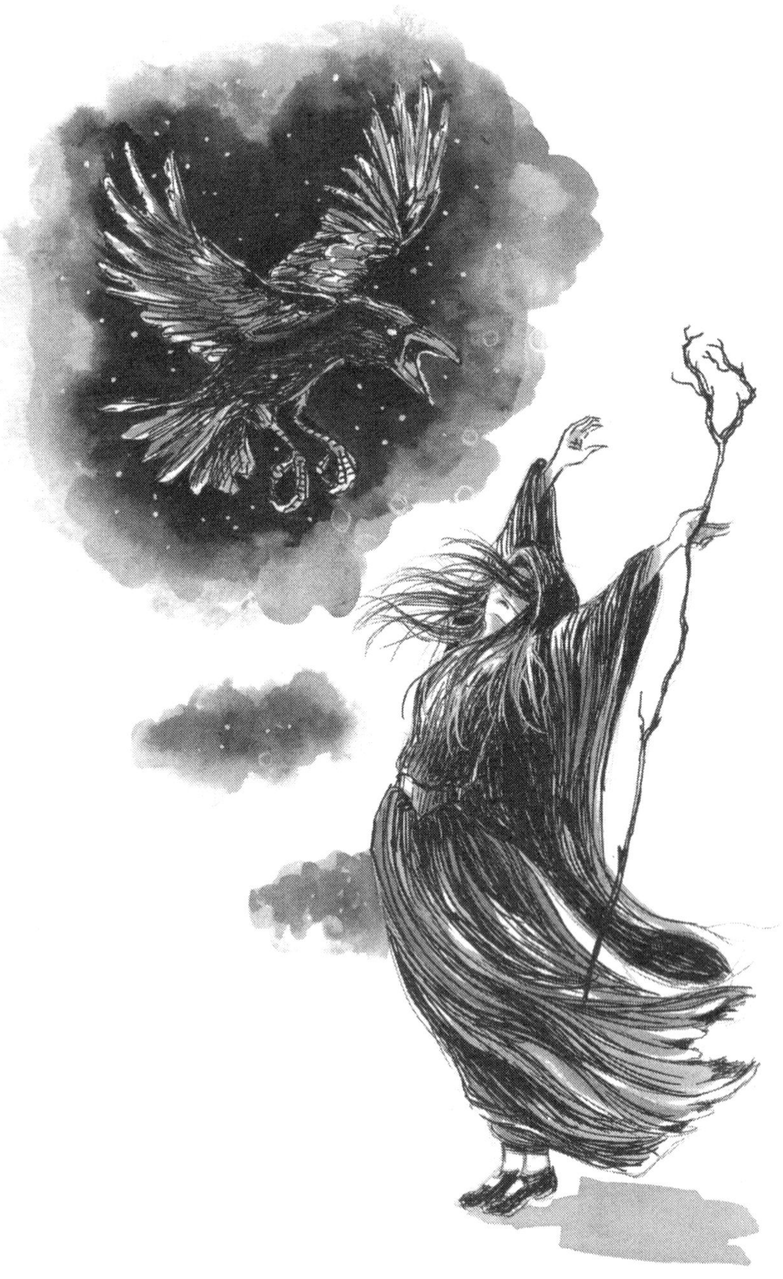

"To the site of the resurrection," Eliza commanded, her voice a murmur that seemed to stir the very fabric of the night. The raven cawed once, a sound that reverberated with dark resonance, before launching itself into the sky, its path guided by unseen threads.

Eliza's presence at the old chateau was inevitable. She had felt the pulsations of dark magic rippling from the site, a signature of Anna's insolence, even before the destruction of Etienne's home. Now, she intended to witness firsthand the power that had emerged from the ashes of a burned love. She followed the raven's flight, traversing the storm-ravaged land with a haunting, floating stride as purposeful as it was silent. The scene unfolded like a dark tableau as she arrived at the edge of the chateau ruins.

Amongst the debris, amidst the blackened timbers and charred stone, Anna stood in her ephemeral form as her real body stood miles away at the ruins of Marchessault Castle. Her visage was pale, her eyes intense with a luminous fervor. Luc's spirit hovered beside her, a ghostly figure wreathed in an ethereal glow, his form shifting and undulating like mist caught in a moonbeam. They both remained at the ruins, but all three were present as specters due to the immense dark forces at play.

The spirit of Luc gazed at Anna with a blend of longing and sorrow, his once-human features now an transitory visage that could barely retain its earthly semblance.

Though marked by the weight of her recent acts, Anna's countenance expressed fierce triumph.
Eliza's arrival was not unnoticed. Anna's head turned slowly, and the intensity of her gaze met Eliza's with a palpable and defiant challenge. "You have come," she said, her voice steady, though it bore the edge of a blade. "To witness my power?"

Eliza's eyes narrowed. Her dark and ancient power surged in response to the challenge. "A bold question," she replied, her voice like the whisper of the abyss. "And a more reckless act. You have indeed stirred the very essence of this place. But do not be so hasty to claim dominion. This was my home long before you arrived. Power is not merely a gift but a burden, a curse that demands mastery and sacrifice. I have shown you this."

Anna's lips curved into a wry smile. "And you, what have you sacrificed to retain your dark throne? Innocent mortals?"

Eliza's expression hardened, her control over her emotions a thin veneer over a fierce rage. "The nature of my sacrifices is of no concern to you," she said coldly. "What matters now is the balance of our dark dominion. Your actions may have unsettled the realm, but do not mistake my tolerance for weakness."

The phantasmal Luc, now fully attentive, drifted closer to Anna. His gaze, though lacking true sight, seemed to follow the interplay between the two witches with a mysterious depth. Anna extended her hand toward Luc's spirit, the magical aura around them intensifying as if in defiance of the encroaching darkness.

Eliza's gaze shifted to the spirit. The sight of Luc's phantasmic form invoked a rare pang of empathy in her heart, a fleeting reminder of the mortal emotions she had long cast aside. He was beautiful and retained his form from hundreds of years ago, which excited her. But it was swiftly eclipsed by her resolve. "We shall see," she said softly to Anna, her voice laced with dark promise. "Whether your spirit or your own life will be enough to sustain you. Power such as yours is but a flicker against the enduring night."

With that, she turned on her heel, her dark robes sweeping around her like the tendrils of a shadow. The black raven, landing on her shoulder briefly, let out a mournful, horrid cry before taking flight once more, disappearing into the boundless darkness.

Eliza strode gently toward Luc and Anna, the two of them on guard for anything. The smile on Eliza's face was for Luc as she moved toward him with a seductive sway of her hips, her beauty unmatched anywhere on Earth.

Luc stood motionless as she stopped inches from him. She leaned in and nuzzled his nose with hers, their lips touching slightly.

Anna watched with no fear from her counterpart. She knew that Eliza was only toying with them.

A tongue extended slowly from Eliza's mouth, and she licked Luc's lips, leaving them wet and glimmering. She then giggled like a young woman after her first kiss. "Yummy, de Mornay. Simply yummy," she said as she backed away.

Ten feet away Luc and Anna watched in horror as Eliza's form changed into an old gray hag with drooping facial features and green eyes raving menacingly. Suddenly her tongue shot out and licked Anna's lips as Anna recoiled slightly, her face pinched into disgust. The elongated tongue left a string of slime that extended from Anna's lips as it retreated back to its mistress. "You, my dear Anna, get a little more from me. Don't forget the first time I touched you under the moon." Eliza licked her lips with lingering slime. "I want more of that. And I will have it," she said with a voice both alluring and wheezy.

As Eliza's form disappeared into nearby shadows, the storm clouds began to gather anew, and the winds carried the scent of coming trials. Anna watched her leave, her expression a mixture of resolve and apprehension. The path ahead was fraught with peril and uncertainty, yet the blaze of her ambition burned bright, illuminating the darkened expanse that lay before her.

In the aftermath of the encounter, amid the shattered remnants of the Chateau de Mornay, a new chapter in the dark witches' saga had begun—one where power and sacrifice intertwined in a deadly dance and where the shadows would unveil secrets yet to be claimed.

Chapter Thirty Two

"Go to the Night of Blood, Anna," the booming woman's voice commanded in her mind, like a dagger stabbing, reverberating throughout her conscience. "Show no mercy in your acts, no remorse for anyone, even him. Your mistress commands you."

Standing with Luc next to the crumbled remains of Marchessault Castle after their encounter with Eliza, Anna's body went rigid, her eyes rolling back. She felt The Dark within her, more powerful than ever, and knew Luc was in danger. "Stay away from me, Luc," she spat out as she entered her bi-location.

The haunting moon hung low in the sky, its silvery light barely penetrating the dense blanket of swirling mist that enveloped the pebble road leading to Chateau de Mornay. Shadows danced from torches, their twisted branches reaching out as if to warn against the dark intentions that brewed in the hearts of the approaching mob.

At the forefront of this ominous procession strode Anna, cloaked in the deep hues of night. Her black hair cascaded like a waterfall of ink over her shoulders, framing a face that bore the weight of centuries, her eyes glinting with an otherworldly light— swirling with ancient knowledge and an unquenchable thirst for the past.

The peasants, armed with makeshift weapons—pitchforks, rusted swords, and torches flickering with fervent indignation—followed her, their faces marked by the grime of despair and the fire of rebellion. They had endured too long the oppressive grip of the aristocracy, and the Chateau de Mornay stood as a monument to their suffering, adorned with gilded façades that gleamed mockingly in the moonlight.

"Here!" Anna's sharp and unearthly, commanding voice rang out, slicing through the heavy air. She approached the wrought iron gate that creaked ominously in the wind, its intricate patterns a witness to the grandeur of a bygone era. It stood resolute against the tide of vengeance, an imposing barrier between the peasants and the apathetic lord who had feasted wantonly during their misery.

With a swift motion, she produced a small, ornate dagger, its blade glimmering with an exquisite green light. The handle, wrapped in dark leather, thrummed with the earth's energy. The peasants halted, their breath mingling with the mist, as they beheld the mysterious witch before them, a creature of legend and dread. She was the one they had feared when they were children. Tales of the witch haunting the streets of Corveau at night were a hundred years old. Yet here was proof of her existence. They cared not for her evil. They had a mission, and she was their leader.

"Stand back," she ordered, her voice a hushed whisper that carried the weight of her power. The air thickened with anticipation, the atmosphere crackling as she knelt before the gate. Her fingers traced the cold metal, whispering incantations that curled through the night like smoke.

"Let the past be unbound," she murmured, each word laced with a spell as old as the stones beneath her feet. "Let the blood of the oppressors spill upon this ground."

At her words, the lock, a twisted and rusted remnant of a forgotten era, shuddered violently as if responding to her call. With a final, resounding crack, it splintered open, the gate swinging wide with a shriek that echoed through the night, signaling the arrival of retribution.

Emboldened by the witch's power, the peasants surged forward, their faces alight with fierce determination. Anna rose, the shadows clinging to her like a second skin, and together, they moved as one—an army of the wronged marching up the stone road to confront their oppressors.

As they approached the chateau, its towering spires loomed above them. The windows glowed with an eerie light, flickering like the dying embers of hope within its walls. Inside, the aristocratic family stirred, their cries echoing like an appetizer against the backdrop of the storm about to engulf them.

Anna paused momentarily, her heart storming emotions—anger, sorrow, and a fierce resolve. She thought of the generations lost, the cries of those who had suffered under the weight of the aristocracy's greed, and her heart ached with their pain. She felt the connection to the land beneath her, to the spirits of the forgotten who rallied behind her, lending their strength to the cause. For a brief moment, her tormented soul remembered Luc and her love for him. She knew what was coming to him and his family, yet she still desired to witness it unfold.

"Tonight, we reclaim what is rightfully ours," she declared, her voice rising above the wind, resonating with the enthusiasm of the past and the present aspirations. "Let the night bear witness to our wrath!"

She spoke as a puppet. The words emanating from her mouth were not hers, which gave her the power to lead the charge.

With those words, they surged forward, the wrought iron gate a mere shadow, far behind them as they crossed the threshold into the realm of their intended victims. The chateau stood before them, resplendent yet sinister, a fortress built upon the ashes of the poor.

Anna knew it would be easy to lead the rabble upon her mistress's command. She knew no reason for her actions, but it must be done because her mistress, The Dark, commanded her.

The first echoes of chaos erupted within the grand halls, the cries of the elite turning to screams of terror. Once a sanctuary of privilege, the walls would soon become a harbinger of reckoning. Anna, the ancient witch, led her army into the maw of darkness, her heart beating in rhythm with the surge of vengeance, the promise of justice igniting the air around them.

And in the depths of that night, amidst the clash of steel and the cries of the fallen, Chateau de Mornay would remain despite a fire raging inside, soon to consume the entire building.

Anna watched from outside as the revolutionaries stormed the chateau, their torchlights setting aflame anything in their path. It was astonishing to witness the event Luc had told her about. She had longed to be present at this very moment, and she was, albeit far beyond any reason the old Anna could comprehend. The Dark commanded her. She had sent Anna to complete the task she had wondered about on the first day she and Brad had met the chateau. She had wondered who let them in?

By the evil bidding of her mistress, Anna led the crowd to storm the de Mornays that night.

She knew what was happening inside. She remembered Luc's pain upon telling her the story. But this new Anna did not care for him or his family. Apathy ruled this line of witches. There could be no remorse for anything in the past, present, or future.

Within minutes, Anna had witnessed the event she had been waiting for. Luc de Mornay's bloody body was dragged out of the front door and slid grotesquely down the steps, his head hitting each one as his tormentors gave no quarter. The witch watched with the chateau flames in her green eyes as his grave was dug before her.

Luc, barely conscious and so close to death, turned his head as he lay on the blood-soaked ground. He saw her. Their eyes met, and the remaining goodness in Anna's heart was extinguished. If a dying man could display one final moment of suffering, Luc did so then. His heart broke as they dragged his body into the grave.

A whisper of pain entered Anna's mind while watching the peasants shoveling dirt on top of him. She approached so she could see him one last time. Something compelled her to witness the final mortal moments of Luc de Mornay, as if she were being guided by an unseen hand pushing her toward the hole in the ground. When she reached it, the horror was palpable: Luc's eyes were open as the dirt from two men shoveling piled on his body. His face never flinched when the ground began hitting his face.

Suddenly, his dried eyes shifted to the side and saw his love Anna one last time, her face frozen and unemotional in his last gasp of smoky air from his burning home.

Chapter Thirty Three

"Anna, wake up!" Luc shouted repeatedly as Anna stood before the ruins of Marchessault Castle, the moonlight shimmering in her black hair. Her eyes were open, yet the green was replaced by white, and she stood still like a statue. Luc moved his hand in front of her face to get her attention, but it was no use. She was amid bi-location, yet Luc couldn't comprehend where she was or, more importantly, when.

Then it hit him. A memory. A face. Her face! She was there that night! She watched him buried! But how? Why would Anna be there during the attack on the chateau?

Luc grabbed her arm to stop her, but her head turned swiftly toward him, and his body was flung twenty feet away, landing with a thud amidst the remains of the castle.

Anna's head swiveled grotesquely back toward the ashes, her white eyes as empty as her forsaken heart.

He sat up and watched as her black hair blew in the breeze, and she continued her mission. The memories of Anna and their love affair endured, but now this—moment of terror as his mortal eyes had caught a glimpse of her just before he slipped away so long ago. The new memory suddenly was just *there*.

After watching Anna complete her mission, Luc saw her eyes return to green, and her gaze caught his. "Why, Anna? Why did you do it?"

"I serve The Dark now. She commanded me. Her reasons are her own," she replied dryly.

"The Dark? What is that?" Luc asked.

"You should know. You were with her for over two hundred years."

Luc's brow furled as it hit him. "She was the other I felt, waiting for—you?"

"Yes. Destiny brought me to the chateau. Everything that has transpired was by her design."

"What we had was real, Anna. It was not by design."

"Luc, our meeting was designed, and everything after as well, even our love—must end," she said coldly.

"But why?" Luc panicked. "I am as strong as Etienne now. We can be together finally with nothing in our way," he pleaded.

"No. I don't love you, Luc. I love nothing. I am nothing and everything at the same time. I implore you to leave immediately before I get angry."

Luc was shattered. "I want to be with you forever, mon amour. I know you still love me. You sacrificed yourself and resurrected me!"

"I told you I love nothing. My mortal heart is dead. I pierced it and lived, proving my immortality."

"I won't leave. Just like you never truly left me," Luc demanded.

"Luc, don't test me. I can end you with only a thought now. No more storms or forces from my hands. A single thought will vaporize your ghostly existence yet again. Spirits are a witch's easiest prey. There is nothing that I can't destroy except perhaps Eliza. I'm serious when I say that you need to leave me. Now."

"I don't know where to go. My home is gone."

"Be happy that you attained what Etienne had—the ability to be free of the confines of a building. You can go anywhere. Go haunt Corveau for all I care."

"How can you be so callous to me?"

Her patience faded, Anna roared back with such fury that her hair flew in an unnatural wind, and her eyes grew grotesquely large, "Because I'm a fucking witch, Luc! I love nothing, I feel nothing, I lust for nothing. I am emptiness incarnate, just like all of my sisters before me. My heart is dead. You mean nothing to me." Her rage shook the ground they stood on.

"I won't leave you, mon amour."

"Yes, you will."

Luc suddenly disappeared.

Chapter Thirty Four

Anna, once a radiant beauty with hair the color of spun gold, now resembled a sickly wraith. Her gray skin hung tight over her bones. Once filled with a gentle blue light, her eyes were now cold and dead green. The transformation was almost complete.

Yet, a flicker of humanity remained, a spark of remembrance that refused to be extinguished. She thought of Brad, her beloved husband, the man she had loved with all her heart. A desire to see him one last time, to speak to him, consumed her.

Le Corveau Inn was her destination. Brad had sought refuge there, a place of shadows and secrets. She knew he was there, haunted by the specter of their past. Disguised in a tattered cloak, Anna approached the inn. The night was dark and stormy, a fitting backdrop for her visit. She felt a chill run down her spine as she entered the inn. The place was filled with a palpable sense of unease, a darkness that seemed to seep from the walls. Anna reveled in it like a dog rolling on the carcass of a cat.

She found Brad's room, a small, dimly lit chamber she remembered, and stopped outside. It was their room the day they had met the chateau. She had fainted in the shower. In her mind's eye, she saw a framed photo of her that Brad had taken when he had left the chateau in madness for California. He had kept it with him, holding out hope to be reunited again. Anna never noticed it had went missing.

Brad sat by the window, staring out into the night. His face was etched with lines of sorrow, his eyes filled with a profound melancholy. Anna saw this vision of Brad just now, as she stood in the hall. She also had seen it two thousand years ago through the line of ancient witches she came from and one hundred years from now from her descendants—but all of them simultaneously.

She stepped into the room, her voice a husky, ghostly whisper. "Brad," she said, her voice barely audible. She also saw Luc in the room, waiting in the background, seemingly frozen and unnoticed by Brad. She had cruelly sent him there to witness her return to her husband.

Brad turned, his eyes widening in shock. He didn't recognize her. The woman before him was a grotesque caricature of the Anna he loved. "Anna?" he stammered, his voice trembling.

Anna took a step closer, her eyes filled with a strange intensity. "I was Anna, but you can now call me Annabeth," she said, her voice changed completely.

Brad recoiled, his face pale with fear. He didn't believe her. This couldn't be Anna. This was another woman, older and faded as if she had lived an entire lifetime. Then he saw it in her eyes, the wisdom and last possible vestiges of remaining humanity within the stranger. His wife was inside, somewhere. She looked at him the way only she could. It was a look just for him. He lunged at her, and their lips met hard. Their hands were on each other's heads and faces, feeling everything they had missed since that brilliant first night in the chateau. "Anna, I missed you. I thought you were dead," he said through their kissing.

"I can never die, dear husband," Annabeth replied, pulling her face away from Brad and making eye contact with Luc, who remained standing in disbelief. Annabeth had staged all of it. She saw the torment in Luc's eyes and reveled in her cruelty.

Brad forcefully pulled her to him by the waist of her cloak, his hand on the small of her back just the way she liked it. His lips pressed hard against her neck as she tilted her head up in ecstasy. She wrapped her arms around his strong neck. With tears forming in his eyes, Brad pushed his hands into her breasts and squeezed them hard. She gasped while her eyes turned to the side and gave Luc an evil grin as he stood by the window, forced to behold the reunion, frozen by the witch's spell.

"Take me, husband," she demanded breathlessly, having forgotten the physical strength of the man she had married. Brad was much stronger than Luc. She desired to show the spirit this strength along with true his love—and heartbreak.

Brad complied and tossed her on the bed, spreading her legs and ripping her gown ferociously. He stopped for a moment when he saw her black pubic hair around her spread lips. Anna, the one he knew, had a small blonde patch just above her clitoris. Just as he was about to protest about the strange changes, Annabeth sat up and grabbed his head with both hands, pulling him into her wetness. She held him there as he lapped at her, burying his face in her hair with his tongue deep inside her pinkness. The witch pulled on his head harder as she moaned a grotesque cacophony of different languages and ancient tongues.

At first Brad enjoyed the passion and familiar taste of his wife, but things took a turn. He couldn't remove his head from between her legs and the flavor went sour. Annabeth held him so tight that he had trouble breathing, and when he did, his mouth filled with vile wetness from the cackling witch. He then gagged as something entered his mouth. He felt it move down his tongue and toward his throat. It was her pubic hair slithering down his throat like worms, constricting his breathing. More hair entered his throat until he choked and dry vomited. Annabeth's strength was bestial and her actions barbaric.

Brad's body choked, groaned, and convulsed before going limp. Annabeth turned to Luc with a merciless grin and remorseless glowing green eyes as he watched in terror.

She finally released her husband's head, his eyes bulging from their sockets. The darkness within her was too powerful and had overtaken her last shard of humanity. While sitting up, her fingers elongated around Brad's neck, doubling their length and flaring like tree branches entrapping the soil for nutrients. With a sickening crunch, Brad's neck snapped, ensuring his death. She released him, and his body thudded on the floor. Annabeth stood over him, her face devoid of emotion. She had killed him, her beloved husband, the man she had once loved with all her heart.

But it was not her choice. The Dark within her, the power she had unwittingly unleashed, had forced her hand. She was a victim, a pawn in a game she did not understand.

With an empty heart, she turned away from Brad's lifeless body and made eye contact with Luc one last time. Le Corveau Inn was no longer a refuge. It was a tomb, a place where the ghosts of the past were laid to rest.

"Mon amour," Annabeth heard Luc say desperately as she walked out the door.

As she left the inn, a storm raged outside. The wind howled, and the rain lashed against the windows. It was a fitting end to a tragic tale, a testament to the power of darkness to consume even the purest of hearts.

As Annabeth made her way down the stone street, her stride masked by the length of the black cloak, rain began to fall hard. She reached back and pulled the hood over her head. As she did, she heard uneven footsteps behind her near the Inn. She turned, but she already knew. It was Brad, with his neck grotesquely protruding around his Adam's apple and severe contusions visible. His tongue hung out as he clumsily sauntered toward her. Nonplussed, she turned away and began walking toward the Chateau de Mornay, their once-happy home. The reanimated Brad followed her, his arms hanging loosely as his legs barely worked in concert to keep up with his wife, his murderer, and his mistress.

The moon a sliver, clouds like smoke,
The wind a whisper, bones awoke.
In crypt of stone, where shadows creep,
The necromancer, secrets deep.
With incantations, low and grim,
She stirred the dust, a ghostly hymn.
The dead arose, with eyes aglow,
A ghastly dance, a chilling show.
From coffins bound, they slowly rise,
With skeletal hands and hollow eyes.
They yearn for life, a fleeting trace,
But bound to serve, in this dark place.
The necromancer, with power grim,
Commands the dead, to serve her whim.
A chilling pact, a dreadful trade,
For life eternal, in the grave.
But shadows lengthen, dawn draws near,
The dead retreat, with chilling fear.
The necromancer, left alone,
With echoes of the spirits flown.
The dead may rest, but their cold embrace,
Still haunts the air, in this forsaken place.

Chapter Thirty Five

The rain lashed against the windows of the police precinct, mirroring the storm brewing within Annabeth. Each drop that struck the glass was a hammer blow against her resolve, each gust of wind a whisper urging her on. But hesitation was not an option. The Dark forbade it.

She stood in the parking lot, a silhouette against the glow of the precinct sign, a cloak covering her head and concealing most of her face. Her gnarled hands trembled with the weight of the spell she began to summon. It was a brutal thing, a twisting of the very fabric of free will, but necessary. These men, especially Inspector Boucher, had trespassed onto her land and too close to her new world. There could be no trace of her presence amongst the authorities of mortals.

A low hum vibrated through the air, a dark melody that only she could hear. Annabeth focused her will, channeling her rage and despair into the spell. The precinct building, a symbol of order and justice, began to vibrate.

Inside, the officers, oblivious to the impending danger, went about their business. Boucher, whose face was etched with the lines of cynicism and weariness, leaned back in his chair, nursing a lukewarm coffee. Another Inspector, his face flushed with anger, barked orders at a rookie, his voice echoing through the sterile corridors.

Suddenly, a wave of nausea washed over them with a palpable silence. Their guns, heavy in their holsters, seemed to throb with an unnatural life. A cold dread, born of an unknown fear, gripped their hearts. They looked at each other, their faces pale and drawn.

Then, the whispers began. Faint at first, barely audible above the hum of the precinct's ventilation system, they grew louder, more insistent.

"Do it," the sinister whispers commanded. "End the pain."

The officers, their minds reeling and each one nursing their own trauma from years on the force, reached for their weapons. Their fingers trembled as they drew the cold metal from their holsters. The whispers grew louder, more urgent, a chorus of unseen voices urging them towards oblivion.

Inspector Boucher, his eyes wide with a terror he couldn't name, stared at the barrel of his gun. The metal felt cold and alien in his hands. He wanted to resist, to fight against the invisible force that was controlling him, but his body refused to obey.

The other Inspector, his face contorted in a grotesque mask of fear, echoed his colleague's movements. The rookie, his eyes filled with a desperate, silent plea, followed suit, as did the handful of other officers in the building.

One by one, the officers raised their guns to their heads. The whispers reached a crescendo, a deafening roar that filled their minds.

"Do it," the voices screamed. "Do it now!"

And then, gunshots, all at the same moment.

Afterward, the only sound was the relentless drumming of the rain against the windows. Annabeth's body was weak and trembling from such a powerful incantation. The spell had taken its toll. She had broken them, these guardians of the law, reduced them to puppets dancing on the strings of her despair. But her power restored quickly as the dead souls within the precinct seemed to enter her body, giving her new life.

As she watched the precinct, now eerily silent, a chilling realization dawned on her. There may still be a file on the mystery of Chateau de Mornay, and she couldn't take any chances. The witch raised her arms and summoned a power from the ancient line of dark witches before and after her. It was within her suddenly—whatever she thought of, she could make happen. The frightening tongues of the ages exploded out of her mouth as her eyes glowed bright green in the shadowy night. The precinct light shut off outside, then all the lights inside extinguished. Finally, the building evaporated into a black mist that exploded into hundreds of ravens flying into the sky, cawing maniacally.

Chapter Thirty Six

Eliza stood at the precipice of transformation. The horrid forest cottage, her sanctuary of shadow, was filled with an expectant hush. A cauldron bubbled, its contents a brew of potent herbs and sinister ingredients, such as pieces of a teenage girl. Above it, strange symbols were etched into the cottage wall, a map for the journey she was about to undertake.

Her reflection in the cauldron's depths was a grotesque caricature of humanity. Eyes of emerald, cold and predatory, stared back at her. Her hair, a raven's wing of black, seemed to writhe with a life of its own. And her form, once statuesque, was now gaunt and ethereal, a mere husk for the spirit that burned within.

She was ready.

With a guttural cry that echoed through the cabin, she began the ritual. Her voice, a rasping croak, wove a tapestry of ancient chants. The air crackled with unseen forces, and the cauldron erupted in a frenzy of green flame. "Oracle of Apollo, come forth," she groaned.

From the depths of the brew, a figure emerged—a woman of ethereal beauty yet with eyes as cold as winter. It was Pythia, the primordial Greek Oracle, Eliza's guide, her spirit summoned from the annals of time.

"You call upon me, child of darkness." Pythia's voice was like the whisper of wind through a graveyard. "What is your desire?"

"Strength," Eliza rasped, her voice barely audible over the storm within the cauldron. "I seek the power to transcend my mortal form, become wind, cross the ocean, and claim what is mine."

Pythia nodded, her ethereal form shimmering. "You ask much, child. But you have walked the path of darkness. You have earned the right to seek greater black power." With a gesture, Pythia reached into the cauldron. A beam of emerald light enveloped Eliza, and a searing pain shot through her body. She felt her bones dissolving, her flesh melting like wax. Terror and ecstasy warred within her. Slowly, a transformation began. Her body shrank, elongated, then dissolved into a swirling vortex of darkness. The dark cottage filled with a wind that howled like a wounded beast. In the center of this maelstrom, Eliza's essence took shape.

A black cloud, ominous and foreboding, emerged from the cauldron. It hovered, growing in size and density. Then, it detached from the ground and soared towards the cottage's mouth.

The floor shook, and the Earth trembled as the cloud erupted through the door into the night sky. It was a creature of shadow, a living embodiment of darkness. As it ascended higher and higher, it transformed into a colossal, menacing shape, a harbinger of doom.

Within moments, the Atlantic Ocean was a vast expanse of inky blackness before the accelerating cloud. Without hesitation, the cloud plunged into the void, disappearing into the night. A new era was dawning, an era of darkness and power. Eliza, the witch, was no more. In her place was a dynamic force of nature, a storm brewing over the horizon.

And in the heart of France, Annabeth, the newly anointed witch, felt a cold shiver run down her spine. A presence was coming, a presence of immense power. And she knew, with a certainty that chilled her blood, that this was no ordinary storm.

Chapter Thirty Seven

Annabeth's white eyes returned to normal as Brad stood next to her, the bi-location complete, her black hair and weathered face now the hallmark of her existence. Annabeth approached the massive pile of ashes and bricks where Chateau de Mornay once stood proudly for hundreds of years.

The moonlight made the white ashes gleam as her black cloak dragged across the spot where she and Brad had happily discussed the sale price of the chateau with Marcel not so long ago. Things had changed. So many things. Gone was her hope for a happy new beginning with her husband, replaced by dark thoughts and a broken heart mended only by evil and its attractive sway to the downtrodden. She used to be Anna, the beautiful blonde with blue eyes and sweetness in her soul. Now, she was Annabeth, Lady of The Dark, with tattered black hair, gray skin, and dark green eyes, all caused by the immense strain of her metamorphosis.

The witch stopped where the stone steps endured, their material resistant to the inferno she had created. The same steps had invited Vivienne Laurent to her fateful final destination within the chateau. Annabeth closed her eyes and vividly saw Vivienne running through the snow and up the steps as the German bullets whizzed by her and slammed into the massive wooden front door. Annabeth was there as Vivienne entered the chateau. The Lady of The Dark watched the Germans lumber toward the steps, one of them spotting her and stopping for a moment. His heart went even colder as he stared transfixed into her hollow white eyes. The evil was within him, murder on his mind, kindled even higher by the witch standing in the snow before him.

"You will be the first to die," her ominous, crackling, pained voice said in German. "She awaits you inside."

The soldier stumbled away after the terror entered him and made his way up the steps to join his doomed companions. He looked back one last time to see Annabeth standing and staring with milky eyes bereft of color, a maniacal tooth-filled smile to haunt him in his final minutes.

Annabeth opened her eyes and saw the pile of ashes again, the brick chimneys enduring, reaching for the starry sky. She began a low chant, whispered and audible only to her and the dark forces surrounding her being. Loneliness was her friend, The Dark grasping onto the pain and giving her the power she desired and harnessed to great effect.

The inferno she had unleashed had wrought devastation upon the majestic Chateau de Mornay, reducing it to a smoldering heap of charred wood and fragmented stone. Yet, amidst the ashes of its former grandeur, Annabeth harbored a vision both magnificent and malevolent—a vision of resurrection and renewal.

The fire, a deliberate conflagration ignited by her hand, had consumed the chateau with an intensity born of her unbridled will. It was a spectacle of destruction, an offering to the dark forces that she then unknowingly served. And now, as the embers cooled and the last vestiges of the blaze were a distant memory, the Lady of the Dark stood resolute, prepared to enact the second part of her dread design.

She began the restoration ritual with a chant whispered in tones that seemed to vibrate with ancient power. The air around her thrummed with evil energy, and the ground beneath her feet pulsed with an ominous rhythm. Shadows danced across the desolate ruins, coalescing into ethereal shapes that spiraled and wove around her in a macabre ballet.

Her voice, a seductive murmur tinged with malice, recited the arcane formulae that would summon the dark forces necessary to do her bidding. The chants, laden with a terrible beauty, rose in crescendo, filling the air with an oppressive weight that pressed upon the very soul. As her words took shape, the remains of the chateau began to stir with an unnatural vitality.

Stone and timber, guided by unseen hands, lifted from the ground and reassembled with an eerie precision. The once-dead remnants of the towers coalesced into an ominous form, rising from the ashes like a grotesque phoenix. The chateau reformed, yet its new visage was far from the opulent splendor of its former self. Instead, it emerged as a dark and forbidding monolith, a testament to the twisted artistry of its mistress.

The walls, now a somber dark gray, loomed high and imposing, their surfaces etched with runes of dark significance. Windows, devoid of light, stared out like hollow eyes, their frames distorted and gaping. The once-grand halls, now cold and shadowed, exuded an aura of evil that seemed to seep from every crevice. The chateau had been transformed into a fortress of The Dark, a sanctuary for the darkness that Annabeth so ardently desired. She knew Eliza would try to claim it. Eliza may have been in the chateau hundreds of years ago, but Annabeth was now the denizen of the powerful nexus of evil, *her* nexus of evil. She would defend it to the end.

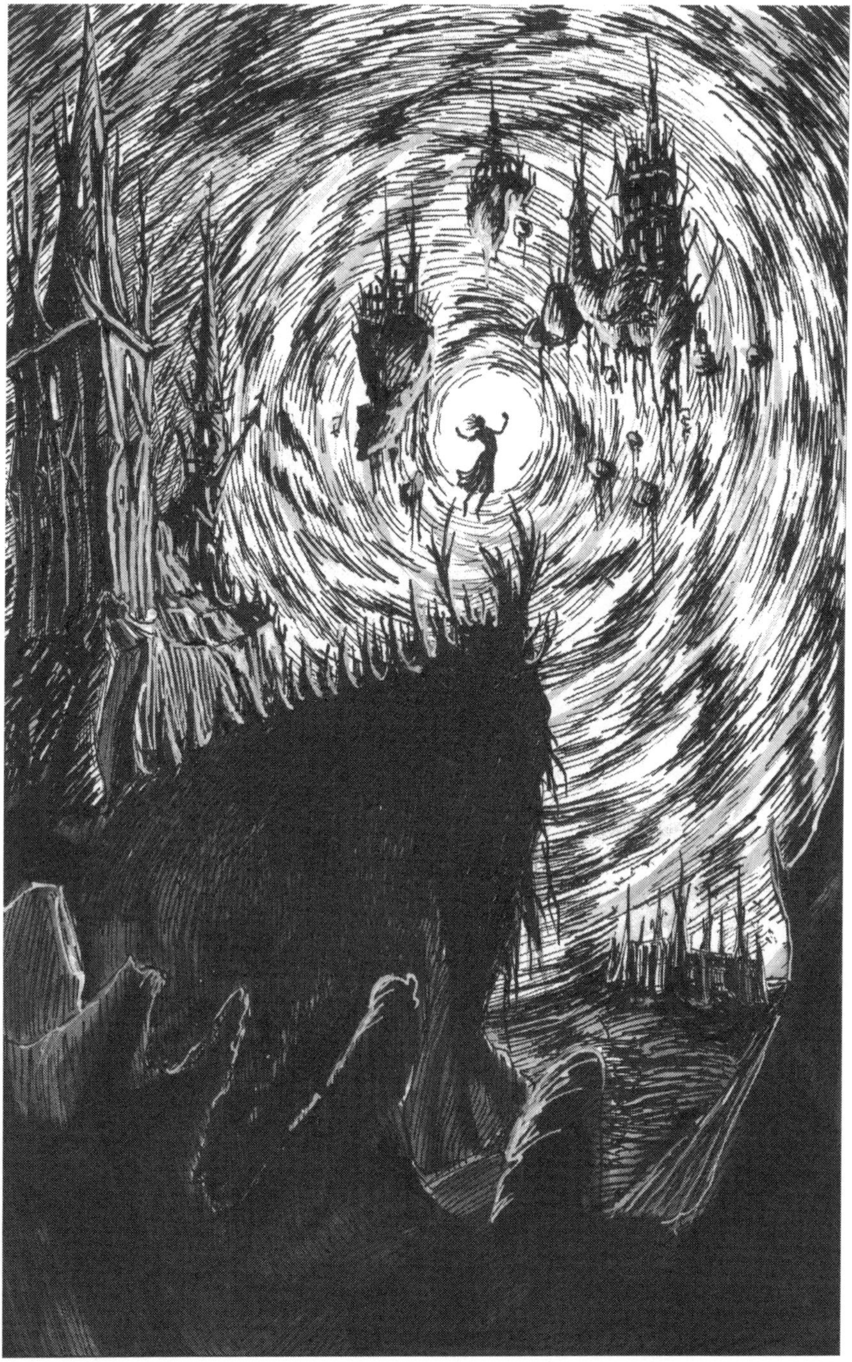

As the final stones were set and the last of the dark enchantments took hold, Annabeth's gaze turned with a sinister satisfaction toward the central chamber of the chateau, where a new scene awaited her.

Her husband, Brad, stood there, bound by the rituals of death and resurrection. His return was a product of her dark sorcery—a resurrection from the very jaws of mortality, a feat that rendered him not a man, but a servile entity bound to her will.

His appearance was wraithlike, his form both familiar and otherworldly. An ashen semblance of existence had replaced the life that had once animated him. Though once warm and lively, his eyes now reflected the cold depths of the abyss in their blackness. His countenance, though recognizable, was imbued with a delicate quality that spoke of his transition from the mortal realm to a servant of The Dark.

Annabeth approached him with a grace that belied the grim nature of their reunion. Her eyes, alight with a fervor born of dark triumph, met his, and a tender and sinister smile played upon her lips. The reunion, marked by the undying bond of their past, was now tainted by the irrevocable shift their destinies had undergone. Brad was no longer merely her husband but a loyal servant, bound to her by the chains of necromantic will.

Now a sanctuary of shadow and dread, the chamber was ready to fulfill its purpose. It would serve as the nexus for her continued machinations, where the dark forces she had summoned could conspire and congeal. The chateau's new form mirrored the twisted grandeur of its mistress—oppressive, dark, and utterly devoid of light. Annabeth reveled in the completion of her dark design as the evening deepened into night, and the chateau stood poised upon the threshold of its new existence.

The Chateau de Mornay had risen from its ashes, not merely as a relic of bygone days, but as a fortress of sinister power, ready to serve the will of its dark sovereign and her newly resurrected consort.

In the depths of the resurgent chateau, as shadows lengthened and the air grew thick with the stench of ancient malice, Anna and Bradley Stone began their new chapter—written in the ink of darkness and sealed with the binding essence of pure evil.

In Chateau de Mornay, there's a tale they say,
Of a woman named Anna, once bright as day.
Her beauty once renowned, her charm so divine,
But darkness consumed her, a witch's design.

Anna's curse, a wicked thirst,
Her beauty turned to darkness, her heart accursed.
She haunts the halls of Chateau de Mornay,
A witch's shadow cast, forever to stay.

Her laughter now echoes in the dead of night,
Her eyes glowing green, a chilling sight.
The walls whisper secrets of her twisted past,
A spell she cast, her beauty did not last.

They say she weaves spells in the pale moonlight,
A haunting presence, a ghostly sight.
The villagers tremble at Anna's name,
For her dark magic brings nothing but shame.

Beware the witch of Chateau de Mornay,
Anna's curse lingers, never to sway.
Her beauty faded, her heart turned cold,
A cautionary tale, centuries old.

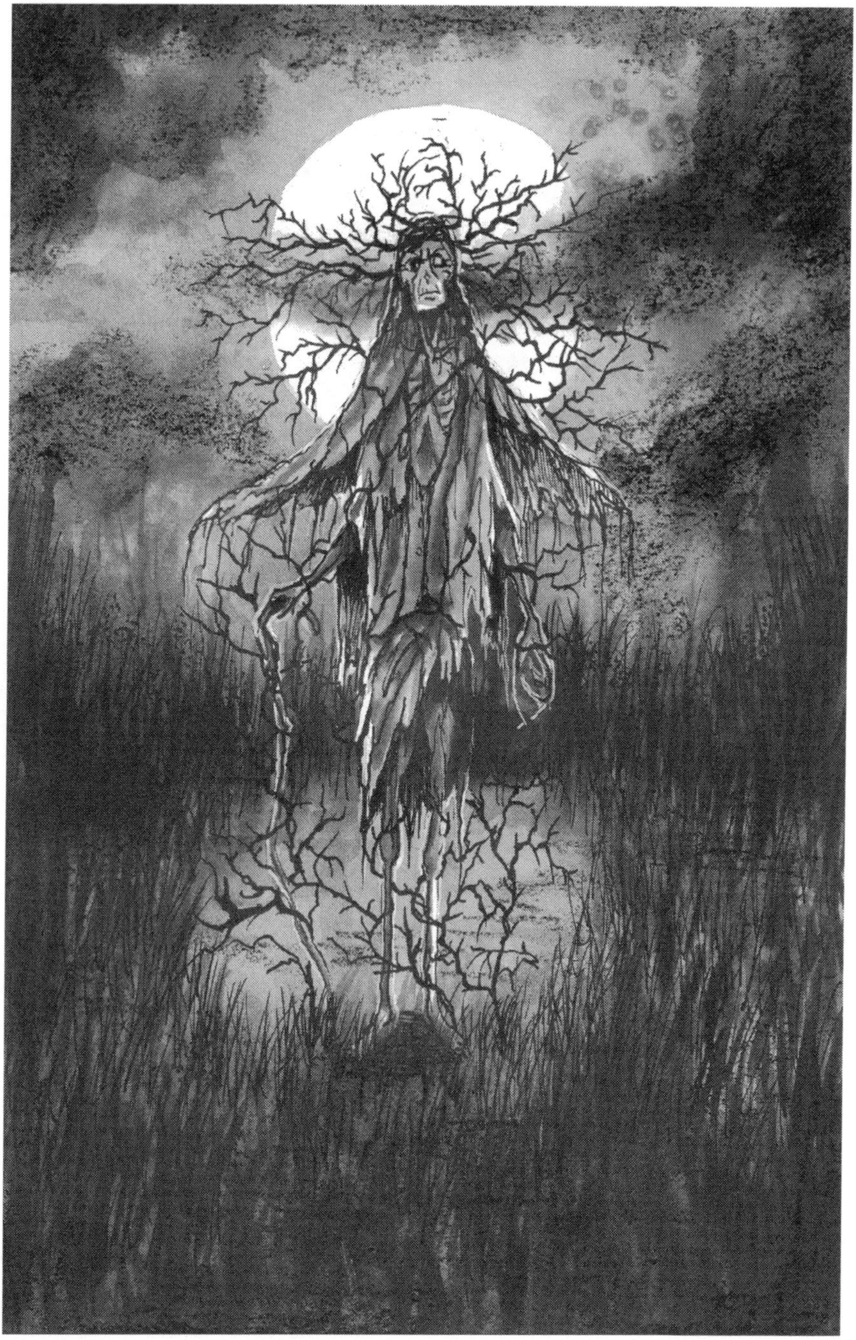

Blake Edward Andrew lives in Eugene Oregon and enjoys spending time with his two children Isla and Max, playing music and video games with them, and teaching them about his love of art, writing, and music. Blake has been writing ever since the second grade, when he penned "The Haunted House", his first foray into his favorite genre of horror. A lover of storytelling, Blake has written several unpublished short stories and movie scripts throughout his life. The Haunting of Anna Stone is his second published novel and the second book in The Haunting Trilogy.

Made in the USA
Columbia, SC
14 April 2025